Alone in the World . . .

Suddenly a loud, long whine met Melissa's ears. She knew instantly that it was the monitor by her mother's bed.

Melissa watched in horror as two white-coated doctors sped to her mother's cubicle, followed by a nurse and an orderly. There were muffled voices, then a louder shout, then nothing but the insistent whine of the monitor.

Frantically, Melissa looked to Andy for hope, but he was leaning against the wall with his back to her, his face buried in his arms.

The doctors emerged slowly, shaking their heads. Suddenly the whine stopped, and for the first time, in the silence that followed, Melissa could hear her brother's quiet sobs.

Bantam Skylark Books in the SWEET VALLEY TWINS AND FRIENDS series
Ask your bookseller for the books you have missed

Sweet Valley Twins Super Editions

Sweet Valley Twins Super Chiller Editions

SWEET VALLEY TWINS
AND FRIENDS

Elizabeth and the Orphans

Written by
Jamie Suzanne

Created by
FRANCINE PASCAL

A BANTAM SKYLARK BOOK
NEW YORK · TORONTO · LONDON · SYDNEY · AUCKLAND

RL 4, 008–012

ELIZABETH AND THE ORPHANS
A Bantam Skylark Book / April 1992

Sweet Valley High® and Sweet Valley Twins and Friends are
trademarks of Francine Pascal

Conceived by Francine Pascal

Produced by Daniel Weiss Associates, Inc.
33 West 17th Street
New York, NY 10011

Cover art by James Mathewuse

Skylark Books is a registered trademark of Bantam Books, a division of
Bantam Doubleday Dell Publishing Group, Inc.
Registered in U.S. Patent and Trademark Office and elsewhere.

ISBN 0-553-15945-3

Published simultaneously in the United States and Canada

Bantam Books are published by Bantam Books, a division of Bantam
Doubleday Dell Publishing Group, Inc. Its trademark, consisting of
the words "Bantam Books" and the portrayal of a rooster, is Registered
in U.S. Patent and Trademark Office and in other countries. Marca
Registrada. Bantam Books, 666 Fifth Avenue, New York, New York
10103.

PRINTED IN THE UNITED STATES OF AMERICA

OPM   0 9 8 7 6 5 4 3 2 1

Elizabeth and the Orphans

One

◇

"How do you get a divorce from your brother?" Jessica Wakefield asked in social studies class Monday morning.

Mrs. Arnette cast Jessica a frustrated look. "Are there any *other* questions about our families project?" she asked. "Helpful, *appropriate* questions?"

Elizabeth Wakefield looked across the aisle at her twin and giggled.

"As I was saying," Mrs. Arnette continued, "this project will show us that a family can be defined in many different ways. Each of you will have a partner from the class who you'll interview. Your job is to meet your partner's family and get to know them. Then you'll deliver a report to the class about what you've learned."

Mrs. Arnette stepped behind her desk and opened a drawer. "You may remember that on your last class project I assigned partners, and there was quite a bit of grumbling."

Elizabeth glanced at her twin sister, remembering their project on the 1920s when nobody had wanted Jessica for a partner. Jessica did a lot of goofing off, which was fine with the rest of the class—unless they had to depend on her for a grade.

Not that Jessica wasn't popular. She was a member of the Unicorn Club, an exclusive group of girls who considered themselves the prettiest and most popular at Sweet Valley Middle School. Jessica was far more interested in boys, clothes, and talking on the phone than she was in grades.

Elizabeth, on the other hand, was an excellent student. On projects like the one Mrs. Arnette had just assigned, everyone wanted Elizabeth for a partner. Not only was she a good student, she was a gifted writer, too. She and her friends had founded *The Sweet Valley Sixers*, the sixth-grade newspaper, and she dreamed of becoming a professional writer someday.

Despite their different personalities, the twins did have some similarities. They were carbon copies of each other with their long, blond hair and blue-green eyes. And they were best friends, as well as sisters.

Mrs. Arnette took a round glass bowl from her desk drawer. "I would like you each to write your name on a piece of paper and place it in this bowl. Then I'll draw names to pair you up. That way you can't blame me if you don't like your partner."

"I feel sorry for whoever picks our names, Elizabeth," Jessica whispered. "They'll get stuck interviewing Steven."

As the students passed the bowl around the room, filling it with little slips of paper, the bell rang.

"Don't even think of moving until I call your name," Mrs. Arnette warned. She reached into the bowl and pulled out two slips of paper. "Amy Sutton," she read. "And Mandy Miller. You two girls may leave." She pulled out the next slip. "Jessica Wakefield," she called, "and Lila Fowler."

"All right!" Jessica yelled. Lila was one of her closest friends and a member of the Unicorn Club.

Several more names were called before Mrs. Arnette got to Elizabeth's. Elizabeth watched Mrs. Arnette ceremoniously unfold the next piece of paper. "Melissa McCormick," she read.

Elizabeth twisted around in her seat and waved at Melissa, a tall, slender girl with long auburn hair and large green eyes. Melissa smiled back.

Elizabeth stood up and gathered her books. She remembered Melissa from Madame Andre's ballet class. Melissa's family hadn't lived in Sweet

Valley very long, and Elizabeth had never gotten to know her very well. She thought that this would be a great chance for them to become friends.

"Hey, Melissa, wait up!" Elizabeth called as she reached the hallway.

Melissa turned around. "Hi, partner," she said.

"I'm glad we're going to be working together," Elizabeth said as they walked down the hall.

"Me, too," Melissa said.

"Hey, Elizabeth. Who'd you get?" Jessica called. She and Lila were standing together by the water fountain.

"Melissa."

"Melissa?" Jessica asked, then she glanced over at Melissa and a look of recognition dawned on her face. "Oh. Well, Melissa, there's good news and bad news. The good news is you'll get to interview me."

"And the bad news?" Melissa asked.

"You'll have to interview my obnoxious brother, Steven, too."

"I'm sure he's not that bad," Melissa said, smiling.

"He's worse. I wish I could trade him in for a new one."

"He's too cute to trade in, Jessica," Lila pointed out.

"What do you know about brothers?" Jessica asked. "I lucked out getting you for a partner, Lila. It'll be a short report! All I have to do is interview your dad."

"Quality is what counts," Lila said. Lila lived alone with her father, one of the richest men in Sweet Valley.

"Do you have a big family?" Elizabeth asked Melissa.

"I have a brother, Andy," Melissa said. "He's a senior. And then there's my mom and me." She paused, looking away. "And, well . . . that's about it."

Elizabeth noticed the pinkness in Melissa's cheeks. "We'll talk about the project later," she said, hoping she hadn't embarrassed Melissa in some way. "Maybe you can come over some afternoon this week and meet everyone."

"That sounds like fun," Melissa said. "Well, I guess I should get going. You know how mad Ms. Langberg gets if you're late to gym."

"Too bad you got stuck with someone so boring," Jessica commented as they watched Melissa walk down the hall.

"How do you know she's boring?" Elizabeth demanded. "We hardly know her."

"If she were worth knowing, we'd know her," Lila remarked.

"That's Unicorn logic for you," Elizabeth said with a wry smile. "Anyway, I'm glad I'm going to get to know her better." But even as she said it, Elizabeth couldn't help feeling that getting to know Melissa might take some work.

"We're doing family reports for social studies class," Melissa said as she walked home with her brother Monday afternoon. Although the middle school was a few blocks away from Sweet Valley High, Andy often walked Melissa home from school when he didn't have basketball practice.

"Family reports, huh?" Andy asked. "Sounds like you'll be snooping around in my fascinating private life."

Melissa took a couple of quick steps to keep up with Andy. He was well over six feet tall, and even though Melissa was tall for her age, she had a hard time keeping up with his long stride.

"We're working in pairs," Melissa told Andy. "My partner is Elizabeth Wakefield. She'll be writing about our family, and I'll be writing about hers."

"Good luck trying to explain our family to anybody," Andy said. "Or should I say, our father. Our *ex*-father."

Melissa glanced at her brother and saw the familiar tight-lipped expression he wore whenever he spoke about their father.

"You know," Melissa said, trying to sound cheerful, "there are some advantages to having a dad who's run off."

"Such as?" Andy asked impatiently.

"Well, think of the money we've saved on Father's Day presents. Not to mention birthdays and Christmases." Melissa paused suddenly. "I just realized his birthday's in a couple days."

"Like he's remembered *our* birthdays in the last four years!"

"I just meant . . ." Melissa hesitated. "I was just surprised that I'd forgotten until now. It's like Dad doesn't even exist anymore."

"He doesn't," Andy said sharply.

Melissa sighed. Andy never wanted to talk about why their father had left or about the bitter fights their parents used to have. Melissa couldn't recall all the details of their fights anymore, but she remembered the doors slamming so hard the paintings on the wall shook. She remembered the angry, sullen dinners, when the only thing breaking the silence was the clink of silverware on plates.

Her parents had been so unhappy. She had begun to think that it was just as well her father had left. She still had the letter he'd written after he'd gone. "I love you kids," he'd written, "but sometimes love isn't enough."

Enough for what? Melissa still wondered sometimes. But she didn't dare ask Andy.

As they approached their house, they saw their next-door neighbor, Mr. Franco, working on his rosebushes like he did every afternoon. In the eight months since the McCormicks had moved to Sweet Valley, the Francos had become their good friends.

"They're beautiful," Melissa told him, pausing to sniff a delicate peach-colored bloom.

"Your mother's volunteered to keep an eye on these while we're on vacation in Europe," Mr. Franco said.

"How long are you going to be gone?" Andy asked.

"Three months," Mr. Franco replied. "We've been planning this trip for years, you know. We've got relatives in Italy, so we'll spend most of our time there. But I intend to get my money's worth on those plane tickets. I've been promising Mrs. Franco a romantic dinner in Paris since we first got married!" He cut two rosebuds and presented them to Melissa. "One for you, and one for your lovely mother."

"Thanks, Mr. Franco," Melissa said. "I'll put them in water right away."

"Mr. and Mrs. Franco are such a happy couple," Melissa said wistfully as they climbed the porch steps to their small house. "I wish Mom and Dad could have been like them."

Andy frowned. "They were like them—once."

"Well, if it isn't my two favorite people!" Mrs. McCormick exclaimed as Melissa and Andy entered the house. She was lying on the couch, an afghan draped over her legs, and her face was pale. Mrs. McCormick had a heart condition that had grown worse over the past couple of years. She'd already been in the hospital twice since moving to Sweet Valley.

"Are you feeling OK, Mom?" Melissa asked as she gave her mother a kiss.

"Just a little tired, honey," she replied. "Mr. O'Neal let me off early from the supermarket. Nothing to worry about." She nodded at the roses Melissa was carrying. "I see you ran into Mr. Franco."

"He's glad you're going to be baby-sitting his roses," Andy said, as he sat down close to his mother.

"I promised him we'd keep an eye on his house while they're gone, too," Mrs. McCormick said. "He's been a little worried since the Nelsons' house down the street was burglarized last month." Mrs. McCormick pushed off her afghan. "I've got to get dinner going or we're all going to starve."

Melissa felt a twinge of worry as she noticed the dark circles under her mother's eyes. "I'll fix dinner, Mom," she volunteered.

"Then we really *will* starve," Andy teased. "I'd better give you some help. You're dangerous in the kitchen alone."

"Fine," Melissa said. "But I get to be head chef."

"And you can be head dishwasher, too," Andy said with a grin.

"Thanks, you two," Mrs. McCormick said, leaning back on the couch. "How'd I end up with such wonderful kids?"

"Don't speak too soon," Andy warned. "Wait and see what the chef here cooks up."

Melissa laughed. "I'm going to go change my clothes. Don't start without me."

As she headed into the hallway, Melissa glanced back at her mother. A cold, familiar fear filled her chest. She hated it when her mother wasn't feeling well.

As Melissa entered her room, her eyes fell on her father's old guitar. He'd learned to play on that guitar as a kid, and it had always been his sentimental favorite. Melissa had thought that there was a reason her father had left it behind. She was sure it meant he was coming back someday.

She reached over and touched the smooth wood. The guitar was like her old pair of roller skates lying nearby—well-worn and too familiar to part with—but no longer useful.

"I really should get rid of that old thing," she muttered.

But she knew she never would.

Two

"Steven has been on the phone for *days*!" Jessica cried in frustration Monday night.

She dropped onto Elizabeth's bed and pulled the pillow over her head. When there was no response from her twin, she let out a bloodcurdling scream and tossed the pillow aside.

Elizabeth sat at her desk, staring calmly at her math homework. "These word problems Ms. Wyler assigned are really tough," she said, tapping a pencil against her math book. "Have you done the one about the two trains going backwards yet?"

"How can you worry about backward trains when I'm having a nervous breakdown?" Jessica demanded.

Elizabeth shrugged distractedly.

"You don't understand, Lizzie," Jessica moaned. "*Your* obnoxious, self-centered brother has been on the phone with his girlfriend ever since we finished dinner!''

"*My* brother?"

"I'm divorcing him."

"I don't think you can do that, Jess."

"I'm sure there's a way. Dad's a lawyer, after all. I'm going to have him draw up the papers." Jessica sighed. "Are you even listening, Elizabeth? You could at least try to be a little sympathetic!"

"I just don't understand why you two have been arguing so much lately," Elizabeth said.

"It's not me—it's Steven," Jessica insisted. "He never gets off the phone, and it's driving me crazy. We were nice enough to set him up with Cathy Connors. After all, if it weren't for our brilliant matchmaking techniques, he'd still be dousing himself with cologne and mooning over Jill Hale. But is he the least bit grateful? *No!* Instead he spends every waking minute on the phone with Cathy, and he won't get off when I need to make very important calls."

"I have to admit Steven is pretty head-over-heels," Elizabeth said.

"Yeah. We made a big mistake, Lizzie. I mean it's absolutely disgusting. What could Cathy possibly see in him? I bet she'd change her mind if she heard one of his deafening after-dinner burps."

Elizabeth giggled. "Or saw the collection of dirty clothes under his bed."

Jessica glanced at the clock. "I promised Lila I'd call her by eight," she said angrily.

"I was hoping to call Amy tonight, too," Elizabeth said.

Jessica jumped off the bed. "If he's still on that phone, this means war."

Jessica stomped out and found Steven sprawled on the floor next to the hall phone. "Steven," she hissed. "Is that thing permanently glued to your head?"

Steven covered the receiver with his hand. "Beat it, shrimp," he said.

"I am sick of you hogging the phone!" Jessica screamed. "And don't call me shrimp."

"You're one to talk, motor-mouth! You were gabbing on the phone most of last night with your stupid Loony-corn friends."

"*Unicorn*, Steven!" Jessica cried in exasperation. But Steven was already back to cooing into the phone to Cathy.

"Excuse me while I go get my barf bag," Jessica called.

She stomped downstairs to the living room where Mr. and Mrs. Wakefield were reading the newspaper. "What is all the commotion up there?" Mrs. Wakefield asked.

"Mom and Dad, you have *got* to do something about Steven," Jessica said, trying to sound calm.

"What exactly did you have in mind?" Mr. Wakefield asked, looking up and rubbing his eyes.

Jessica sat on the arm of the couch. "I thought maybe you could send him to military school."

"Jessica!" Mrs. Wakefield exclaimed, laughing.

"OK, then. But you've got to punish him," she said.

"Punish him for what?" Mr. Wakefield inquired.

"For being *Steven!*" Jessica cried. "For hogging the phone for hours on end so Elizabeth and I can't make vital phone calls related to schoolwork."

"I had a feeling this was going to be about the phone," Mrs. Wakefield said. "It seems like this fight has been going on for weeks."

"Exactly!" Jessica said.

"And I'm tired of it," Mrs. Wakefield said with a sigh. "Why can't you two get along? I haven't seen you fight like this since you were two-year-olds."

"And it's all his fault," Jessica muttered.

"As far as I'm concerned, you and Steven are old enough to figure this out on your own, Jess," Mr. Wakefield said. "Instead of fighting like cats and dogs, why don't you try something sensible, like making a schedule?"

"A schedule?" Jessica repeated doubtfully.

"Assign phone times, and then stick to them," Mr. Wakefield said.

"I think that's a wonderful idea," Mrs. Wakefield agreed.

A phone schedule? *Maybe it isn't such a bad idea, after all,* Jessica decided.

Especially if *she* was the one who made it.

"What is that thing you've been working on?" Lila asked the next day at the Unicorner, the table where the Unicorns always gathered for lunch.

"It better not be homework," Janet Howell warned. Janet, an eighth grader, was the president of the Unicorns. "You know we don't allow homework at the Unicorner. It's bad for our image."

"Jessica, doing homework at lunch?" Ellen Riteman, another sixth-grade Unicorn, cried. "Give me a break!"

"This," Jessica said, waving a sheet of paper in the air, "is the answer to my problem."

"Which one?" Janet asked, laughing.

"Steven." Jessica pointed to the page, which she'd neatly divided into little squares. "He's been driving me crazy lately, especially when it comes to the telephone. He practically *lives* on the phone."

"Phones are far more important to girls than to guys," Ellen said. "It has something to do with hormones, I think."

"Ellen's right," Lila agreed. "I remember that from science class. You know, I tried to call you twice yesterday after school, Jess," she added as she opened a carton of milk. "It was busy. I'll bet it was Steven."

Jessica sighed. "Steven tied up the phone blabbing with Cathy Connors all night! You should hear them talk baby talk to each other!"

Ellen smiled dreamily. "How romantic!"

"You mean, how revolting," Jessica snapped.

"But you and Elizabeth helped set them up," Mandy Miller said.

"I wouldn't have, if I'd known it was going to destroy my social life," Jessica replied. She waved the paper. "That's why I made this—a phone schedule. Actually, it was my dad's idea." She set the chart in the center of the table. "I divided the day into half-hour pieces. Then I assigned blocks of time and colored them in. See? Elizabeth's blue, Steven's brown, and I'm purple, of course."

Purple, the color of royalty, was the Unicorns' official color. They all tried to wear at least one item of purple clothing every day.

"How come there are hardly any brown squares?" Mary Wallace asked. "I'm not sure Steven's going to go along with this idea, Jess."

"He has fewer squares," Jessica admitted, "but they're better squares." She pointed out a small block of brown near the bottom of the page. "See? I gave him all the best evening stuff."

Janet peered closer. "Jessica!" she exclaimed.

"Who's going to talk on the phone at four in the morning?"

Jessica shrugged. "Steven's older. He usually stays up later than Elizabeth and I do."

"Has Elizabeth seen this chart?" Belinda Layton asked. "I don't see much blue on here, either."

"That's because Elizabeth doesn't use the phone as much," Jessica responded. "I have more of a social life than she does."

"Well, I'm glad I don't have to deal with any brothers or sisters," Lila said.

"I'm glad you don't either," Jessica joked. "Otherwise I'd have a lot more work to do on that stupid families project."

"Tell me about it!" Belinda moaned. "I got stuck with Tommy Fishbourne. He's got *nine* brothers and sisters! My report's going to be the size of a book!"

"That's even worse than Elizabeth," Jessica said with a laugh. "She's got Melissa McCormick. How boring can you get! But at least Melissa only has one brother."

"One very cute brother," Janet said. "He's the star of Sweet Valley High's basketball team."

"Hmm." Jessica tapped her finger on her chin. "Maybe I should ask Steven about him."

"See, Jessica?" Belinda said. "Older brothers are good for some things."

Jessica sighed. "I guess." She looked back

down at her chart. "Does anybody have an eraser?" she asked. "I see a square I'm going to steal from Steven."

"Isn't that Melissa McCormick up ahead?" Elizabeth asked as she and Amy Sutton, her closest friend, left the lunchroom and headed down the hall. "Melissa!" Elizabeth called.

Melissa turned around and smiled. "Hi," she said.

"Amy and I were just talking about the families project at lunch. I was thinking maybe you could come over to my house this weekend so we could get started on it."

"That would be great," Melissa said. "I—"

"Melissa McCormick!"

The girls turned. Mr. Clark, the principal, was hurrying toward them, his face grim.

"I don't know what I've done, but it doesn't look good!" Melissa whispered, a nervous smile on her face.

"Melissa, I need to talk to you for a minute," Mr. Clark said.

"Sure," Melissa said, casting a nervous glance at Elizabeth and Amy.

"We'll wait for you over by our lockers, OK?" Elizabeth said.

Melissa nodded and followed Mr. Clark into an empty classroom nearby.

"I wonder what that was all about?" Amy

said. "Melissa doesn't exactly seem like the type who'd be in trouble with the principal."

"I don't think she's in trouble," Elizabeth whispered. "Mr. Clark's expression makes me think it was something else."

"Like what?"

"I don't know," Elizabeth answered. Suddenly she heard a sob echo down the long hallway.

Melissa emerged from the classroom with her face buried in her hands. Mr. Clark had his arm draped around her shoulder, as if he were trying to comfort her.

"I wonder what's wrong?" Amy asked as Mr. Clark led Melissa quickly down the hall.

When she neared Amy and Elizabeth, Melissa paused. Her green eyes were shiny with tears. "It's my mom," she said in a soft, choked voice. "She had a heart attack. She's in the hospital."

"Oh, Melissa—" Elizabeth began, not knowing what to say.

"I have to go," Melissa said softly. "I have to go see her right away."

Three

◇

"Got your seat belt on?"

Melissa nodded and gazed blankly at the inside of the car. Mr. Clark's station wagon was old and smelled like a dog. There were gold tufts of fur all over the seats.

"This old battleship's seen better days," Mr. Clark said brightly as they pulled out of the middle school parking lot. He paused, glancing over at Melissa.

She could feel his eyes on her, but she couldn't think of anything to say.

"Sorry about the fur," he said. "We've got a golden retriever who loves to sit in the front seat."

Melissa plucked at a piece of wide gray tape that stretched the length of the front seat.

"She's going to be OK, Melissa," Mr. Clark said suddenly, his voice quiet.

Melissa nodded again. *She's going to be OK,* she repeated to herself silently.

When they reached the hospital parking lot, Melissa jumped out of the car and dashed toward the main entrance. As soon as she was inside, the smell hit her so hard she gasped for air. She'd almost forgotten the harsh odor of sickness and antiseptic.

When Mr. Clark arrived in the lobby, he asked for directions from the receptionist.

Melissa leaned against the wall, feeling woozy. She should have prepared herself for that hospital smell. She'd been here twice before, after all. This wasn't the first time her mom had been sick. It wasn't even the first time she'd had a heart attack.

In a way, Melissa felt reassured. Her mom had been sick before, and she'd always gotten better. It had always turned out OK. She hoped that it would be OK this time, too.

"This way," Mr. Clark said, tapping her lightly on the shoulder. "She's in ICU. That's—"

"I know," Melissa said quietly. She knew all about the intensive care unit, with its tubes and beeping machines and nurses and doctors who never looked you in the eye.

"She's going to be OK," Melissa said as they entered the elevator.

Mr. Clark looked down at her. "You bet she is," he said softly.

The door opened and Melissa was halfway

down the hall when she heard Andy's voice. She ran to him and flung herself into his arms. "She's going to be OK," she whispered.

Andy drew back a little. "Of course she is," he said. "Have you seen her yet?"

Melissa shook her head and pulled away. They hadn't hugged like that in a long time. Not since the last time they'd been at the hospital.

"Come on," Andy said. "Let's go see Mom."

Melissa glanced behind them at a short blond woman talking quietly with Mr. Clark. "Who's that you came with?"

"The vice principal. Ms. Hollingsworth."

They approached a high desk where a nurse sat. Behind her was a long wall with glass windows. And behind the glass, Melissa knew, were the patients. There were white curtains pulled around the beds, with doctors and nurses scurrying back and forth.

"Melissa?" the nurse asked. "Is that you?"

Melissa managed a smile. She remembered Carol from the last time her mother had been here. She'd brought Andy and Melissa pillows when they'd spent the night on the plastic waiting room couches.

"I'm so sorry to see you two back here," Carol said kindly.

"Can we see her?" Andy asked.

Carol glanced at one of the curtained cubicles. "Let me check," she said.

Melissa watched the nurse disappear behind the first white curtain. She reached for Andy's hand and squeezed it.

Moments later, Carol returned. "Just for a few minutes," she said. "Your mom is very weak. She needs to save her strength."

She led them through the door. A bearded doctor emerged from Mrs. McCormick's cubicle. He was studying a chart as he passed them.

Carol pulled the curtain back and for a brief second Melissa closed her eyes. *No matter what you see*, she told herself, *don't react*. She couldn't let her mother see any worry in her face.

But when she opened her eyes, fear knifed through her, and she had to swallow a gasp. Her mother lay there, eyes closed, her face gray against the pillow. There were tubes everywhere, more tubes than Melissa remembered ever seeing before. Behind her a glowing green monitor beeped.

For a moment, Melissa focused only on the little jumping dot traveling across the screen. Each one was a heartbeat, and each heartbeat was a sign of hope. *She's going to be OK*, she told herself. But somewhere in her heart she knew that things were worse this time.

Mrs. McCormick opened her eyes. Andy reached for one of her hands, and Melissa took the other. They felt weightless and frail.

"I'm glad you're here," Mrs. McCormick said

in a voice that was barely a whisper. She closed her eyes, then opened them again. "I'm so sorry, kids."

"Sorry for what, Mom?" Andy asked. "You can't help being sick. It's not your fault."

Melissa looked over at him and saw the sheen of tears in his eyes. She knew how hard he must be fighting to keep control. Andy hated to cry.

"I want you two to promise me something," Mrs. McCormick said. "Something that will make me feel a lot better." Suddenly she paused, her eyes shut, and Melissa knew she was waiting for a spasm of pain to pass. She squeezed her mother's hand, feeling useless and terrified.

Finally Mrs. McCormick opened her eyes again. "I want you to promise me that you'll be good to each other," she said, struggling with each word. Slowly she turned her head toward Andy. "Take care of your sister, Andy."

"I will," he promised.

"I love you both very much," Mrs. McCormick said. She smiled a smile that made Melissa's heart wrench. It was a peaceful smile, one that said, *I'm giving up now.*

"I love you, Mom," Melissa said, tears spilling down her cheeks.

"I love you, too, Mom," Andy echoed, but Mrs. McCormick's eyes had already closed, and she seemed to be sleeping soundly.

Andy moved to leave. But Melissa couldn't seem to let go of her mother's hand.

"Come on, Lissa," Andy said hoarsely.

Gently Melissa released her mother's hand. She paused at the curtains and turned. The monitor still glowed green. The slow steady beeping was strangely reassuring.

Carol was waiting outside. She led Melissa and Andy to a small waiting area nearby.

"She looks so frail," Melissa said softly.

"She's stronger than she looks, honey," Carol replied. "Why don't you two head on down to the cafeteria and have some of our world-famous mystery casserole? There's nothing you can do here right now. Your principals are down there having coffee."

"I'm staying right here," Melissa said firmly.

"Me, too," Andy agreed.

Melissa slumped onto the cold plastic couch. Her body was shaking. "What if?" she blurted suddenly, surprised at her own voice. "What if something happens?"

"Nothing's going to happen," Andy said sternly. "Nothing."

Carol sat down next to Melissa and hugged her. Melissa was grateful for her comforting.

"We'd be all alone in the world," Melissa said, and a deep uncontrollable sob swept through her. "We don't have anyone but Mom. No one."

"Stop it, Melissa!" Andy nearly shouted.

Then, more quietly, he added, "We have each other."

Suddenly a loud, long whine met Melissa's ears. She knew instantly that it was the monitor by her mother's bed.

"I have to go, sweetie," Carol said as she jumped to her feet. "You stay here."

Melissa watched in horror as two white-coated doctors sped to her mother's cubicle, followed by Carol and an orderly. There were muffled voices, then a louder shout, then nothing but the insistent whine of the monitor.

Frantically, Melissa looked to Andy for hope, but he was leaning against the wall with his back to her, his face buried in his arms.

The doctors emerged slowly, shaking their heads. Suddenly the whine stopped, and for the first time, in the silence that followed, Melissa could hear her brother's quiet sobs.

Four

$\Diamond$

"I want you both to know how very sorry I am about your loss," Mr. Clark said as he drove Andy and Melissa home from the hospital.

Melissa sat stiffly in the back seat. Neither of them answered. It must have been the thousandth time Mr. Clark had said those words.

Melissa stared at the tissue she'd shredded into little bits in her lap. She hadn't cried since they'd left the hospital. She hadn't talked, either.

She looked at Andy sitting in the front seat, staring straight ahead. He had only sobbed those few moments. Then he'd stopped. After that, he'd been calm and reasonable and adult. It should have been reassuring, but it made Melissa feel even more alone.

Melissa looked out the window and watched the familiar buildings rolling past. The Sweet Valley Mall. The skating rink. The Shop and Save, where her mom worked as a cashier.

Someone would have to tell Mr. O'Neal, her mom's boss. Someone, but who? She tried to imagine picking up the phone. *"Hello? Mr. O'Neal? I'm calling to tell you my mom won't be coming back to work. Ever."*

Mr. Clark cleared his throat. "I, um, I'm afraid I don't know a lot about your family, Andy," he said quietly. "You haven't been in Sweet Valley that long, and I haven't really had a chance to get to know you folks."

Andy nodded.

"I was wondering if there's anyone you'd like me to contact."

"Contact?" Andy repeated dully.

"You know, about your mom. I understand from the hospital that she didn't ask them to contact your dad when she was admitted. I could call him for you now, if you like."

Andy turned to face Mr. Clark. "No," he said sharply. "I'll take care of all that."

Mr. Clark adjusted his tie with one hand. "I'd feel better if I knew—"

"He's out of town on business," Andy said quickly. "But he'll be home tonight."

"Oh," Mr. Clark said. "That's settled, then." Melissa thought he sounded relieved.

For a moment Melissa imagined what it would be like to have her father home again, but she knew it was pointless. He was gone. He could be two miles away, or a thousand. He could be anywhere. It didn't matter.

Nothing mattered anymore.

Other thoughts marched through Melissa's mind, but nothing seemed to stick. It was as though her whole body had gone numb.

"Is there anyone else you'd like me to call?" Mr. Clark asked as he pulled up in front of the McCormicks' house. "A relative to stay with you until your dad gets home this evening?"

"We'll be fine," Andy replied. He reached over and shook Mr. Clark's hand. "I want to thank you for all your help today, sir."

"If there's anything I can do, you just pick up the phone," Mr. Clark said kindly.

Andy got out of the car and opened Melissa's door. She stepped into the bright sunlight and squinted. *It should be raining*, she thought angrily.

"You take care, Melissa," Mr. Clark said.

Melissa nodded. "Thank you," she said softly.

At the front door, Andy pulled out his key and paused. Mr. Clark was still waiting in the driveway to be sure they got in safely.

Suddenly Melissa couldn't bear the thought of being in the house without her mother there. "I can't," she whispered.

"It's OK, Lissa," Andy said gently. "It'll be OK."

They stepped inside the house and Andy closed the door behind him.

"She can't be gone," Melissa whispered to Andy. "She can't."

They sat down on the couch together and Melissa pulled her mother's afghan around her. Although it was a beautiful, warm day, she'd been shivering ever since she left the hospital.

"Why did you lie to Mr. Clark about Dad?" Melissa asked.

"I had to," Andy replied. "Or they'd split us up."

"They?" Melissa echoed, feeling a rush of fear.

"Social services," Andy said. "Since I'm only seventeen." He draped his arm around her shoulders. "Don't worry, Lissa," he said softly. "I'm going to take care of you now."

But who will take care of you? Melissa thought.

All afternoon and into the night Andy and Melissa sat together, huddled on the couch. When the phone rang, they didn't bother to answer it. Andy turned on the TV after a while, but they left the sound off. The house was eerily quiet, and Melissa had never felt so empty.

"Andy, there's someone at the door," Melissa said groggily Wednesday morning. She opened her eyes and was surprised to see the bright morning sun streaming through the living room picture window.

There was another knock at the door, this time louder.

Andy stood and stretched. His clothes and hair were rumpled. For a brief moment Melissa couldn't remember why they'd slept in their clothes on the couch. Then it hit her—*Mom is dead.*

Andy pulled open the door. Mrs. Franco was standing there with a plate of cookies. "Why, hello, Andy," she said, surprised. "I just finished making Mr. Franco's favorite cookies, and—" she paused, peering inside. "Why aren't you two in school? Is it some kind of holiday?"

Andy cleared his throat. "Come on in, Mrs. Franco," he said quietly.

Mrs. Franco stepped inside and placed the cookies on the coffee table. She looked from Andy to Melissa and back again, her brow knitted. "It's your mother, isn't it?" Mrs. Franco said softly, reaching for Andy's arm. "Has she had another heart attack?"

Andy bit his lower lip. "She died yesterday, Mrs. Franco," he replied.

"Oh, you poor children!" Mrs. Franco murmured as her blue eyes welled with tears.

"Here, sit down, Mrs. Franco," Andy said, leading her to the couch where she settled next to Melissa.

Mrs. Franco wiped away her tears and wrapped her thin arms around Melissa. Melissa let herself cry again, softly, as Mrs. Franco rocked back and forth.

"Your poor mom," she said. "We didn't know her long, but Mr. Franco and I were so fond of her."

Andy sat down in the easy chair. "She liked you, too, Mrs. Franco," he said. "You were her closest friend here in Sweet Valley."

"She never talked much about herself," Mrs. Franco said, shaking her head. "I knew she had some health problems, but she never complained, never let on that she was feeling poorly."

Just then there was another knock at the door. Andy sighed and went to open it.

On the porch stood a middle-aged woman with short graying hair. She was carrying a blue folder. "Andy McCormick?" she asked.

"Yes."

"My name is Sarah Scott. I'm from the child protection division of the county social services office."

"And?" Melissa heard him say curtly.

"May I come in?"

He hesitated, then opened the screen door.

Ms. Scott stepped into the living room and glanced around curiously.

"This is Mrs. Franco," Andy said. "Our next-door neighbor. And that's my sister, Melissa."

"Hello," Ms. Scott said. She smiled at Melissa. "I'm very, very sorry about your mother."

"How do you know about our mom?" Andy demanded.

"A nurse at Sweet Valley Hospital informed us," Ms. Scott said.

"But why?" Andy asked.

"She was concerned about your welfare," Ms. Scott replied. "She seemed to think you wouldn't have any adult supervision."

Carol, Melissa thought. She thought of Andy's words last night. Could Ms. Scott be here to split them up?

"We're perfectly fine," Andy said, pacing across the living room. "Everything's under control." But the sound of his voice told Melissa that Andy was frightened.

"I can assure you we have your best interests at heart," Ms. Scott said kindly. She pulled a pencil out of her purse. "I just need to ask you a few simple questions. I know this is a bad time, but it will only take a few moments." She opened her folder. "Now, I'm assuming your father is deceased?"

"No!" Melissa cried without thinking.

Andy shot her a warning look. "Our father is traveling overseas, Ms. Scott. He'll be back soon."

Mrs. Franco looked confused. "But your parents are separated, Andy—" she began.

"That doesn't matter," Andy said firmly.

"As soon as we contact Dad, he'll make arrangements for us to live with him." He paused. "That's how they planned it. In case anything ever . . . happened."

For a moment Melissa's heart raced. Could it be that Andy actually knew where Mr. McCormick was? But as quickly as the thought came to her, it vanished. Andy was just trying to get rid of the social services lady.

"What will you do in the meantime?" Ms. Scott asked as she scribbled something down in her folder.

"I'll take care of Melissa," Andy answered. "We'll be just fine. I *am* seventeen," he added.

Ms. Scott smiled. "I'm sure you'd do an excellent job caring for your sister, Andy. But you're still a minor. The state requires that you and your sister have some form of adult supervision." She smiled at Melissa. "We have some wonderful temporary foster homes. Nice people you can stay with until your father returns."

Foster homes? Melissa stared at Andy in disbelief.

"We are not going to a foster home," Andy said in a determined voice. "We are staying together, right here."

"I'm afraid you don't have a choice, Andy," Ms. Scott said firmly.

"Of course they do!" Mrs. Franco said suddenly. "Suppose the children stayed with us until their father arrives? We'd love to have them." She hesitated. "Of course, we're going on a long trip in another week, but your dad will certainly be home by then, don't you think, Andy?"

Andy nodded. "Oh, sure," he said confidently. "As soon as we get in touch with him, he'll fly straight here." He smiled, a wry smile that only Melissa could understand. "Dad'll drop anything when it comes to us kids."

Ms. Scott hesitated. "Well, I suppose that would be acceptable, Mrs. Franco, if you're certain about this."

Mrs. Franco gave Melissa a hug. "Of course I am. It's settled."

"And you'll have your father notify me as soon as he gets to Sweet Valley?" Ms. Scott asked Andy.

Andy nodded. "Of course."

Ms. Scott dug through her purse. "Well, here's my card, then. If I don't hear from him within a week, I'll get back in touch so we can make arrangements with a foster home before the Francos leave."

Five

◇

"Well, I guess that's enough stuff," Melissa said that afternoon as she crammed a pair of pajamas into her suitcase.

"I don't know why you're packing all this," Andy said as he stood in her bedroom doorway. "It's not like we're going far. You can come over here whenever you need anything."

"I don't want to come back here," Melissa said firmly. "It doesn't feel like our house anymore. Not without—" she stopped suddenly, then she took a deep, steadying breath. Melissa decided that if Andy could be brave, then she could, too.

"Here," Andy said gently. "Let me help you close that thing. You've got enough clothes in there for three suitcases."

Melissa watched as Andy slowly zipped the suitcase shut. "Andy?" she asked quietly. "What are we going to do when the Francos have to leave and that social services lady finds out Dad's not coming?"

"I'll think of something, Lissa," Andy said.

"We'll think of something together," she said.

She helped Andy drag her suitcase into the living room. When they heard a knock at the door, they both stopped in their tracks. "Now what?" Andy wondered aloud as he went to the door.

When Andy opened the door, Melissa was surprised to see Elizabeth Wakefield standing there.

"Melissa," Elizabeth began quietly. "I tried to call you last night . . ." Her voice trailed off.

"Come on in, Elizabeth," Melissa said awkwardly. She hardly knew Elizabeth, and it seemed strange to see her now, when school seemed a million miles away.

Elizabeth stepped inside.

"Andy, it's Elizabeth Wakefield," Melissa said.

"Hi," Andy said. He turned to Melissa. "I guess I'll take this suitcase over."

Without Andy in the house, Melissa felt completely abandoned. What could she say to somebody like Elizabeth—a normal person, with two parents and no problems in the world?

"I just wanted you to know how sorry I am about your mom," Elizabeth said gently. "Mr.

Davis told us what happened this morning in homeroom."

"Thanks," Melissa said weakly.

"I know we don't know each other that well, but I wanted to say that if there's anything I can do—" Elizabeth shrugged helplessly. "I mean, like bringing you your homework until you feel like coming back to school. Or if you need someone to talk to, maybe."

"Thanks, Elizabeth," Melissa said, her voice quaking slightly. "It was really nice of you to come by. But I'll be back in school soon." Until the words were out of her mouth, Melissa realized she hadn't even thought about returning to school. It seemed so unimportant now.

"Are you going away?" Elizabeth asked.

"Away?"

"Your brother was carrying that suitcase."

"Oh. We're just staying with our next-door neighbors for a few days until—" Melissa paused, remembering Andy's lie—"until my dad gets back from overseas. He does a lot of business there, and we haven't been able to get hold of him." Now that the lie had started, she couldn't seem to stop. "We haven't seen him in a long time," Melissa continued. "Years, in fact. My parents were separated, but he's coming back and everything will be fine as soon as he gets here."

For a moment, the girls were quiet. "Well, I guess I should be going," Elizabeth said, breaking the silence. "I'll call you soon to see if you need anything, OK?"

"We'll be at the Francos'," Melissa said. "They're in the book." Even though she hardly knew Elizabeth, she felt better knowing she'd be calling. "Thanks, Elizabeth," Melissa said softly. "Really."

"Mom, Steven is driving me crazy!" Jessica cried Wednesday afternoon.

Mrs. Wakefield dropped a bag of groceries on the kitchen table. "Jessica," she said wearily, "don't start. I just walked in the door. And I had a tough day at work."

"Mom, I wouldn't bother you unless this was really important," Jessica said. "Steven refuses to follow my telephone schedule. You know—the one you and dad suggested I should make?"

Mrs. Wakefield kicked off her shoes and began to fill a teapot with water. "Is the schedule fair?" she asked.

"Fair?" Jessica said as she peered into the grocery bag.

"Did you divide the time up evenly?"

Jessica hesitated. "I gave us each the amount of time we need, depending on our social lives."

Mrs. Wakefield put the teapot on the stove and shook her head. "And just how did you determine that?"

Jessica shrugged. "Well, you know Elizabeth.

She barely uses the phone, compared to me. Mostly she talks to Amy and Todd. Whereas I have a lot more friends."

"And that means more phone time."

"I knew you'd understand," Jessica said. "Now Steven barely needs the phone at all, since he's a guy. And there's no point in him making goo-goo talk to Cathy all night, when he sees her every day at school, anyway."

Mrs. Wakefield sank into a kitchen chair. "Jessica, enough. I'm going to let you figure this out on your own."

"But—"

"I don't want to hear the words 'Steven' or 'telephone' come out of your mouth for the next month. Got it?"

"Got it." Jessica sighed and headed to the family room, where Steven was on the couch, talking on the phone, and Elizabeth was sprawled on the floor working on her English homework.

Jessica picked up her phone chart from the coffee table.

"No one's going to follow that schedule, Jess," Elizabeth murmured, her eyes on her English textbook. "Not as long as you get nineteen hours out of every day, I get three, and Steven gets two."

"But I gave you the six to seven slot, Lizzie," Jessica protested, pointing to a blue square on the chart.

"That's when we have dinner, Jess."

Jessica rolled her eyes. "You're so picky, Elizabeth. Do you have any idea how difficult it was to make this schedule?"

"Hey," Steven said, his hand over the receiver, "could you two please keep it down? I'm trying to have a conversation here."

Jessica glared at him. "Do you see this square, Steven?" she asked. "This is a *purple* square. You are not purple. *I* am purple. You are brown. Get it?" Jessica glanced at her watch. "For the next forty-two minutes, that telephone belongs to me."

Steven grimaced. "Says who?"

"Says this chart."

"And when, exactly, can I use the phone, according to your little chart?"

Jessica smiled with satisfaction and scanned the chart for a brown square. "Here," she said. "You can call Cathy then."

Steven peered at the chart. "Hey, Cath," he said into the phone, "set your alarm for four A.M., OK? Cause that's when my deranged little sister's letting me use the phone."

"Give me that phone, Steven," Jessica commanded.

"Forget it, shrimp," he growled. "And you can forget that idiotic schedule."

"Steven!" Jessica cried, her voice rising. "I need that phone now to call my friends!"

"The Candy-corns will just have to wait," Steven replied.

"*Unicorns!*" Jessica shouted. She stomped over to the phone, grabbed it from Steven, and hung up on Cathy.

"You want to play dirty, Jess?" Steven cried. "Just to spite you, I'm going to call Cathy right back, and I'm going to stay on the phone all night. Till, say, four A.M. *Then* you can have it!"

Jessica let out a moan. "Elizabeth!" she cried. "Do something!"

Elizabeth gathered up her homework and stood. "I am," she said calmly. "I'm going upstairs where I can get some work done. You two are acting like preschoolers."

Jessica stared at her brother, who was redialing Cathy's number. "This means war, Steven Wakefield!"

Six

◇

"It's too bad your father couldn't attend the funeral," Mrs. Franco said Friday afternoon. "It was such a lovely service."

Melissa nodded stiffly as she settled onto the Francos' living room couch. She and Andy, the Francos, and Mrs. McCormick's boss from the grocery store were the only people at the funeral. Melissa had read a poem she'd written that her mom had always loved, but halfway through she'd started to cry and Andy had to step in and finish it for her.

Melissa glanced around the room. Mr. and Mrs. Franco were both dressed in black, and Andy had on his navy blue suit that was a little too small for him. Melissa had worn a dress her mother had made for her last year, a bright splash of colorful flowers on a blue background. Somehow that had seemed better than black.

"Anyway, if your father could have attended the funeral, I'm sure he would have thought it was lovely," Mrs. Franco continued.

Melissa had a feeling she knew what was coming next. She had grown used to Mrs. Franco's prying by now. In the two days since she and Andy had been staying there, they'd managed to dodge most of the questions about their father's whereabouts.

"You know," Mrs. Franco said, taking a seat next to Melissa on the couch, "your mom never spoke much about your father, except to say they'd separated a few years back." She paused, waiting for a response, but Andy looked out the window, lost in his own private thoughts, and Melissa just folded and unfolded a napkin.

Mrs. Franco tried again. "Come to think of it, I never really asked—what exactly does your father do for a living?"

"He's a musician," Melissa answered.

"Sales," Andy said at almost the same instant.

Melissa cast a nervous glance at Andy.

"He sells music," Andy said quickly. "You know—he writes songs, then other people record them."

"My, how interesting," Mrs. Franco said as she poured herself a cup of coffee out of a silver pot.

"That's a beautiful coffee pot," Melissa commented, hoping to change the subject.

"It belonged to my grandmother," Mrs. Franco said. "In fact, there's a whole tea service, though we hardly ever use it." She turned to Andy. "Has your father written anything I might have heard?"

Andy shrugged uncomfortably. "Probably not. He writes popular music—you know—"

Mr. Franco chuckled. "He means, not the kind us old fogies would be likely to recognize, Helen."

"Have you ever heard 'Sierra Lullaby'?" Melissa asked. It was a song her father used to sing to her when she was little. Melissa knew the story about her father selling music was just a story and nothing more, but she was enjoying the fantasy.

"I'm sorry, dear, I can't say I've ever heard of that song," Mrs. Franco said.

There was a long silence. At last Andy spoke. "I want to thank you for helping with the funeral arrangements, Mr. Franco," he said, using what Melissa had begun to think of as his "responsible voice."

"No problem, son. I was happy to help," Mr. Franco replied. "And fortunately, her insurance fund covered all the costs."

There was another pause, even longer this time. "Well, I guess I'll go try to get in touch with Dad again," Andy said, getting up. "I left a message at the hotel he was supposed to be staying at yesterday, but I think he may have already checked out."

"Where was that?" Mrs. Franco asked.

"London," Melissa replied at the same moment Andy said, "Vienna."

"No, Melissa," Andy said sharply. "Remember, he was going to Vienna over the weekend?"

"Oh, yeah," Melissa said quickly, feeling her cheeks burn.

"Andy, I keep telling you you're welcome to use our telephone," Mrs. Franco said.

"Thanks, Mrs. Franco," Andy said. "But you've already done so much for us. Long-distance phone calls are expensive, and there's no reason not to use our phone, since it's right next door."

Especially since they're imaginary calls, Melissa thought to herself.

"Well, you run along then," Mrs. Franco said. "I thought we'd have barbecued chicken for dinner, if that's all right with you two."

"Sounds great," Melissa said. The truth was, she had barely eaten since Tuesday. Most of the time, she secretly fed her meals to Mrs. Franco's toy poodle, Francis. Melissa just didn't seem to have an appetite anymore.

Melissa followed Andy outside. "I'll wait out here for you," she said.

"You're going to have to go back in the house

eventually," Andy said gently. "Besides, we need to talk."

"I don't want to go in there," she said firmly.

"Lissa, please," Andy said. "It's important."

Melissa saw the worried expression in his eyes and relented. Andy was right. She couldn't hide at the Francos' forever.

"We'll just go sit in the kitchen," Andy promised. "We need to talk privately."

Melissa nodded.

The house was hot and stuffy. Melissa felt a throb of pain in her chest as soon as she stepped in the door, but she closed her eyes and followed Andy to the kitchen table. *Be strong,* she told herself. *Be strong like Andy.*

Andy took a deep breath. "We can't keep lying to the Francos much longer, Melissa. If we don't come up with a father in the next couple days, social services will put us in foster care. They might even split us up for good. As far as the state's concerned, we might as well be orphans."

Another wave of pain washed over Melissa. She was barely holding on as it was. Life without her brother would be unbearable.

Andy reached for her hand. "I have a plan, Lissa. It's not perfect, but it's our best chance at staying together. Are you with me?"

"What kind of plan?"

Andy looked away. "I know this guy," he

began. "Sam Hughes. He was on the basketball team with me for a while, until he got thrown off for fighting. Anyway, Sam's willing to help us out."

"Help us how?" Melissa asked nervously.

"He's going to pretend to be Dad."

Melissa narrowed her eyes. "How, exactly?"

"It'll be fine," Andy said, sounding as though he were trying to convince himself. "Sam'll call the Francos and Ms. Scott at the department of social services and give them the story. You know, 'this is Mr. McCormick, thanks for looking after my kids, I'll be home any minute now.' No sweat."

"And what does this Sam guy get out of the deal?"

Andy frowned. "Fifty dollars."

"Fifty?"

"I know it's a lot of money, Melissa, but that's the deal. And it's worth it if we can stay together, isn't it?"

Melissa forced a smile. "Yeah, I guess you're worth fifty bucks."

Andy grinned back.

Melissa ran her finger along the edge of the dusty table. "Andy?" she said quietly. "Are we going to be OK? About money, I mean?"

"Sure," Andy said confidently. "I've been doing some figuring. There's a fair amount of money left in Mom's checking account, and we have the automatic teller card and her code number. That means we can take out the money without any questions from the bank. Plus, there's the extra cash she kept in the house for emergencies." He smiled dryly. "And if this isn't an emergency, I don't know what is."

Melissa couldn't help smiling, too. They were going to pull this off, one way or another. She felt sure of it now.

"Melissa?" Andy asked. "I was wondering. Have you thought about going back to school?"

"Not really. How about you?"

"I thought I'd wait until we got everything straightened out with the Francos and social services. We've only missed a few days, and we're both good students."

Melissa looked at the floor. "I don't think I'm quite ready to go back."

"OK," Andy said. "Let's give it a little longer." He smiled. "But not *too* much longer."

"Come on," Melissa said. "It's almost time for dinner. Let's go feed Francis."

"Are you sure you don't want me to get you any homework assignments?" Elizabeth asked Melissa that evening on the phone.

"No. That's OK. But thanks anyway." Melissa's voice was quiet on the other end. Elizabeth could tell her new friend was barely holding back tears.

"Well, I'm glad to hear you'll be back at school soon," Elizabeth said. "And Melissa?" Elizabeth paused. "Um, call me if you feel like talking, OK?"

She hung up the phone and sighed. There was nothing she could say or do to make Melissa feel better. She knew Melissa needed time to grieve and to sort out her feelings.

She tried to imagine what it would be like to lose her own mother, and the very thought brought tears to her eyes.

"Elizabeth? You OK?" Jessica asked as she climbed the stairs. She was carrying several pieces of posterboard.

"I was just talking to Melissa McCormick," Elizabeth said, wiping away a tear. "I feel so sorry for her. Can you imagine what she must be going through?"

Jessica paused, thoughtful for a moment. Then she seemed to shake off the thought. "I don't even want to think about it, it's so awful. Anyway, there's no point in dwelling on it, Elizabeth. There's nothing you can do. You hardly know Melissa."

"Still, I—"

"Could you give me a hand with these signs?" Jessica interrupted. She tossed a roll of tape to Elizabeth. Then she placed one of the pieces of posterboard on her door. "Is this centered?" she asked.

"What exactly is that sign supposed to mean?" Elizabeth demanded.

On the white cardboard was a big red circle with a diagonal slash drawn through its middle, just like a no smoking symbol. But instead of a picture of a lighted cigarette in the middle, there was a crude drawing of a boy. His face was covered with pimples and two of his teeth were blacked out. A phone receiver was growing out of his left ear. On his T-shirt, which had sweat stains at the armpits, was a big letter S.

"Don't you get it?" Jessica asked. "This sign means this area is officially a Steven-Free Zone." She paused to admire her artwork. "I should have added a few more zits, I think."

Elizabeth stared at her sister in disbelief. "Steven never goes in your room, anyway, Jessica. This is ridiculous!"

"It's the *principle* of the thing, Elizabeth."

Elizabeth tossed the tape back at her twin in frustration. "I'm not in the mood for this, Jess," she said with a sigh.

"Well, you don't have to get all high and mighty about it, Elizabeth," Jessica said, insulted. "Especially after I was thoughtful enough to make one for your room, too."

Elizabeth didn't answer. She went to her room and closed the door tightly. At that moment all she wanted was a Jessica-Free Zone.

Seven

"Do you need any help packing, Mrs. Franco?" Melissa asked the next afternoon.

Mrs. Franco looked up from the pile of her husband's socks that she was sorting. "Sit down, Melissa," she said seriously, motioning to a kitchen chair. "We need to talk."

Melissa sat down reluctantly. She wished that Andy were there, but he'd left a couple of hours ago to meet with Sam Hughes.

"Sweetheart, you know how fond Mr. Franco and I are of you and your brother," Mrs. Franco began. "And if there were any way we could postpone our vacation, we would. But we've been scrimping and saving for this trip for years, and the tickets can't be refunded at this late date."

"I understand, Mrs. Franco," Melissa said, anticipating what was coming next. "And Andy and I are so grateful for all you've done for us this week. It's really meant a lot to us. But you don't have to worry about Andy and me. I'm sure we'll get hold of my dad any day now, and we'll be fine until he gets here. Andy left a message for Dad at his hotel in Vienna just this morning."

Mrs. Franco shook her head regretfully. "I just can't leave you here alone, in all good conscience. That woman from social services already called here once this week to see if your father had come back yet."

"Ms. Scott?" Melissa asked nervously.

"I didn't mention it because I didn't want to upset you two. Goodness knows you've already been through enough." She looked up at Melissa. "Aren't there any other relatives you could call, dear? Or maybe a family friend? Just someone who could keep an eye on you until your dad gets here?"

Melissa shook her head. "Nobody. We don't have any relatives, really. And we haven't been in Sweet Valley long enough to make any really close friends."

"You've moved around a lot these last few years, haven't you?"

"Mom was always looking for better work," Melissa said. She shifted uncomfortably in her chair and glanced at the clock on the stove. It was nearly four. That meant, with any luck, all Mrs. Franco's questions would soon be answered.

"It breaks my heart to say this, dear," Mrs. Franco continued as she rolled a pair of socks into a neat ball, "but I'm afraid I'm going to have to call Ms. Scott and let her know the situation."

"Please, Mrs. Franco," Melissa pleaded. "You know how responsible Andy is. He's practically eighteen, after all. We'll be fine alone for a couple days until my dad gets here."

"I can't take that kind of responsibility upon myself," Mrs. Franco said, shaking her head.

"But—" The phone rang, and Melissa turned to stare at it. *Saved by the bell*, she thought. She crossed her fingers, watching Mrs. Franco reach for the telephone.

"Hello?" Mrs. Franco said. She paused, her face clouded. "Could you speak up? I can barely hear you."

Long moments passed. Suddenly her face blossomed into a smile. "Mr. McCormick!" She gestured to Melissa excitedly. "I can't tell you how relieved I am to hear your voice!"

Melissa remembered just in time that she was supposed to look happy. She leaned forward in her chair and pasted a smile on her face.

"Yes, the children are both holding up very well," Mrs. Franco continued. "I'm so sorry about your wife. She was a lovely woman." She paused again. "What's that? I can barely hear you, there's so much static on the line."

Melissa wondered how Sam was managing that sound effect when he was only a few miles away.

"So you'll be home Monday evening?" Mrs. Franco asked. She clasped her hand to her heart. "I can't tell you what a relief that is. Why, I thought I was going to have to hand these poor children over to the county! Mr. Franco and I are leaving on a trip Monday afternoon, but I'm sure the children will be OK by themselves for just a few hours." She paused. "What's that? Oh yes, they're very responsible.

"Well, of course, you're very welcome," Mrs. Franco continued after a pause. "I'm glad we could be of some help." She glanced at Melissa. "Before you hang up, I'm sure Melissa would like to say hello."

Melissa's mouth dropped open in horror.

"Well, come on, dear," Mrs. Franco urged. "It's long distance, after all."

Melissa stepped over to the phone and accepted the receiver hesitantly. *Please don't make me do this*, she pleaded silently. But it was too late, and she knew it.

"Dad?" she said nervously, as Mrs. Franco stood nearby, beaming.

"Hey there, cutie-pie," came a throaty voice on the other end. "How about a kiss for your old dad?"

Sam sounded older than seventeen, Melissa

thought. Then she realized he was probably deliberately lowering his voice.

"Yes, I'm fine," Melissa said, although Sam was laughing on the other end.

Suddenly there was the sound of a scuffle and a muffled shout. "Melissa?" Andy asked breathlessly. "Sorry about that."

"That's OK, Dad," Melissa said. She glanced over at Mrs. Franco and smiled.

"Do you think she bought it?" Andy asked.

"Everything's fine here," Melissa replied evenly.

"Great," Andy said, relief in his voice. "I'll be home soon. Hang in there, kid."

"OK," Melissa said as the line went dead. She paused for a moment, listening to the humming line. The sound reminded her of the droning monitor at the hospital. She closed her eyes.

"I love you too, Dad," she whispered before hanging up.

"Let's see," Mrs. Franco said, consulting her list one last time as she climbed into the car Monday morning. "We've got our tickets and our bags. We're going to drop the dog off at my sister's on the way to the airport. I guess that's everything."

"Let's go, Helen, or we'll never make it to the airport!" Mr. Franco urged, tapping his fingers on the steering wheel.

Mrs. Franco leaned out the window and gave Melissa one last kiss. "Now you'll be sure to pick up the mail for us, and water Mr. Franco's roses?"

"I promise," Melissa vowed. "But I warn you, I don't exactly have a green thumb."

"Your mother did," Mr. Franco said. "I'm sure you will, too."

There was an uneasy silence. "Well, have a safe trip," Andy said at last. "And thanks again for everything, really."

Mrs. Franco wiped away a tear with a hankie. "Take care, kids," she said, squeezing Melissa's hand. "I realize we've only known you a short time, but you're practically like family to us now."

As Melissa watched the Francos' car roll slowly out of the driveway, she was surprised at the tears welling up in her eyes. Suddenly she felt terribly alone, even with Andy standing right by her side.

"I can't believe it," Andy said, shaking his head. "We pulled it off! Ms. Scott and the Francos really bought Sam's act." He nudged Melissa. "Hey, don't you get it? We're free. No foster homes, no social workers, no more Francos."

Melissa nodded slowly. She stared at the house and picked up her suitcase. "Well, I guess it's time to move back home," she said softly.

The house was eerily still. Melissa dragged her suitcase into the bedroom and began to unpack. She turned on the radio in her room to chase away the silence.

"Melissa," Andy said, appearing in the doorway a few minutes later. "I thought we'd have a meeting."

"A meeting?"

"Yeah. You know—like Dad used to have in the old days." Andy turned and headed for the kitchen. Melissa followed behind uncertainly.

There was a large pile of bills on the kitchen table. "I was just going through these," Andy said, settling into a chair. He glanced at a yellow pad of paper with numbers on it. "There are a lot of hospital bills, but most of those will be taken care of by Mom's insurance."

Melissa shivered. She wasn't sure she was ready to hear all this yet. They'd only been back in the house a few minutes.

"And of course, there aren't any mortgage payments," Andy said briskly. "That's one good thing."

"Mortgage?" Melissa echoed.

"You know, house payments. Mom used all of the money Grandpa Harris left her when he died to buy this place."

"Oh," Melissa said weakly. She'd never really given such things much thought.

"What are those pink envelopes?" she asked, pointing to a small separate pile.

"Phone and electricity bills," Andy said.

"They're overdue, so we'll have to pay them soon."

"How?"

Andy patted Melissa's arm gently. "Don't you worry about all that. We've got the checking account money and the emergency cash. And I'm going to take care of all the bills." He nodded, as though he were trying to convince himself of something. "From now on, I'm in charge, OK?"

"OK."

"I think it's time for both of us to get back into a routine, don't you? We'll already have a lot of catching up to do at school."

Melissa nodded. She dreaded going back to school and having to answer all the questions about why she'd been absent. But she couldn't mope around the house forever.

"I'm going to look out for you now," Andy vowed. "Make sure you do your homework and take your vitamins."

Melissa groaned. "And wash behind my ears?"

"I mean it, Lissa," he said. His tone was soothing, almost like a parent would sound. "You can count on me. I'm going to take care of you now." His mouth tightened. "And not like dad, either. I'm going to stick around and make this work. You'll see."

Andy's eyes were filled with sincerity, and Melissa wondered if he saw the doubt in hers. Could they really make this work? *We haven't got a choice. We have to make it work,* she told herself firmly.

"You know, I'm not a kid anymore," Melissa said. "I'm going to take care of you, too." She stood and put her hands on her hips. "When's the last time you washed behind *your* ears?"

She couldn't be certain, but Melissa thought she saw the slightest hint of relief in Andy's smile.

Melissa lay in bed that night, staring at the fluorescent green numbers on her clock radio. 1:47, it said.

Once again she tried to close her eyes and sleep. But every time she did, she saw the steady green blink of the monitor in her mom's hospital room. It would beep a few moments, then flatten into a long green line.

Melissa's eyes flew open. She had never felt so alone, so afraid, or so angry.

Why? she wondered for the hundredth time. Why had her mother left them alone like this? Why hadn't she taken better care of herself? How many times had Melissa asked her to work fewer hours? Hadn't she volunteered to take on a part-time job in the afternoon? Hadn't Andy wanted to work at that fast food place? But her mom wouldn't hear of it. School comes first, she'd kept saying.

Melissa felt a familiar deep sob fill her chest. Maybe if she'd gotten a job, her mother wouldn't have worked so hard. Maybe she wouldn't have gotten sick and left them here to fend for themselves, so completely alone.

She shivered. It seemed like she'd been cold all night. Melissa kicked off her covers and leapt out of bed. She went to find an extra blanket in the hall closet.

Melissa walked slowly down the hall, her eyes adjusting to the dark. She could hear Andy's steady breathing as she passed his room.

That was Andy, all right. Steady. Strong. Why wasn't *he* feeling angry and abandoned? How could he be so sure everything was going to work out?

Suddenly she paused. She was in front of her mother's door. They'd kept it closed since her death, ignoring it as they passed by.

Melissa's fingers touched the doorknob shakily. Gently she pushed open the door. The sweet scent of her mother's perfume made her tremble. The bed lay unmade, the sheets tangled, and a book lay open on the dresser.

Melissa closed her eyes and breathed deeply. Then she crawled into her mother's bed and pulled the covers around her, feeling, at last, like sleep might come.

Eight

◇

Melissa flung open the doors to the lobby at Sweet Valley Middle School and breathed in the fresh air. Mary Wallace, a seventh-grade Unicorn, passed by her and paused. "Melissa?" she said. "Uh . . . I just wanted to say—" Mary hesitated.

"I know," Melissa said, managing a smile. "Thanks, Mary." It was amazing how quickly the news of her mom's death had spread, Melissa thought. It was always the same—people looking away when they met her eyes, teachers taking her aside after class to offer their condolences. She'd said "thank you" to so many near-strangers, she'd lost count.

What Melissa most wanted was to rush home and tell her mom about her day, like she always did. Instead, of course, she would go home to an empty house.

"Melissa?"

Melissa turned around to see Elizabeth Wakefield and Amy Sutton. "Hi," she said, glad to see it was them. They were the only people who'd come close to treating her normally today.

"I know this has probably been a tough day for you," Elizabeth said, "but I was wondering if maybe you'd like to come over to my house this afternoon. Amy's coming, too."

Melissa smiled. "You must have read my mind. I was dreading going home, to tell you the truth. Andy has basketball practice, so he won't be home till much later."

To Melissa's relief, they talked about school all the way to the Wakefields' house. There weren't any awkward questions about Melissa's dad or comments about her mom.

That is, until they got to Elizabeth's house. A few minutes after they settled around the pool, Jessica and Lila appeared.

They stepped onto the patio, each carrying a glass of lemonade. "Oh," Jessica said as soon as she noticed Melissa. "Uh, hi, everybody. We just got back from a Unicorn meeting."

Melissa wasn't surprised at Jessica's reaction. Jessica was one of the people who'd seemed to avoid her all day.

Lila looked nearly as uncomfortable as Jessica. Then, to Melissa's amazement, Lila motioned to her. "Hey, Melissa, come here a minute," she called.

"Watch out," Amy warned with a smile. "Unicorns can bite!"

Melissa walked over to Lila, who pulled her aside. "Look, Melissa," Lila said, "I know we're not exactly friends or anything, but . . ." She ran her fingers through her thick brown hair. "Well, I wanted to tell you I was sorry about . . . you know."

Melissa almost smiled, in spite of herself. She knew Lila Fowler was rarely tongue-tied.

"See," Lila continued, lowering her voice, "I don't exactly have a mom, either. I mean, I do, but she left my dad when I was really young. So in a way, I think I know how you must be feeling. Sort of." She sighed. "Life can really be crummy sometimes, you know?"

Melissa nodded. "I know."

Lila glanced over at Jessica, who was sitting by the edge of the pool, dangling her feet in the water. "If you ever need to talk or anything," Lila said, nearly whispering, "we could." She paused. "Not—you know—in school or anything."

"Thanks, Lila," Melissa said. "I appreciate the offer." *And it's the thought that counts*, she added to herself.

Melissa returned to Amy and Elizabeth. "What was that all about?" Amy asked.

Melissa smiled. "They want me to join the Unicorns," she said with a long-suffering sigh, "but I told Lila they'd have to work on their wardrobes before I'd consider joining. I absolutely *despise* purple."

Amy and Elizabeth laughed, and, for the first time in days, so did Melissa.

"What's so funny?" Jessica asked as she and Lila pulled up two more pool chairs to join them.

"Long story," Elizabeth replied, grinning at Melissa.

"You know what I was thinking?" Jessica said, turning to Lila. "There's a three-day weekend coming up pretty soon. Middle school and high school teachers have meetings all day. What if we had a pool party then?"

"Hey! Who drank all the lemonade?" Steven yelled before Lila had a chance to respond. He strode onto the patio with Joe Howell, his best friend. "I should have known," Steven said, shaking his head. " 'The mouth' got to it first."

"It wasn't just me, Steven!" Jessica protested. "Elizabeth and her friends drank some, too!" She looked at Lila. "See what I mean? Isn't he obnoxious?"

"Hey," Joe interrupted, "who's your new friend, Elizabeth?"

Melissa felt her cheeks begin to burn. She

couldn't believe such a good-looking older guy had even noticed her! Instantly she felt guilty. How could she get excited over something so unimportant? Her mother had just died!

"Melissa McCormick," Elizabeth said, "this is Joe Howell, Janet's older brother."

"And that's Steven," Jessica added. "The one I warned you about."

"Do you have a brother named Andy?" Joe asked.

Melissa nodded proudly.

"No kidding?" Steven said. He was clearly impressed. "Andy's the best center the Sweet Valley varsity basketball team's ever had."

"Andy practically learned to dribble before he learned to walk," Melissa responded. "My dad made Andy a little basketball hoop when he was only four—" Suddenly she stopped. *Don't talk about Dad*, she reminded herself. *It'll just get you into trouble.*

"Anyway," Jessica said loudly, "as I was saying, we could invite all the Unicorns to the pool party. And Elizabeth's friends, too—"

"Hold it right there, shrimp," Steven interrupted. "Just when exactly is this pool party of yours?"

"Why do you care? You're not invited," Jessica responded.

"Well, as long as it's not on that Friday

they're having teacher meetings," Steven said. "Joe and I are going to have a *major* pool party that day."

"Says who?" Jessica asked. "Did you ask Dad and Mom yet? I'd stay away from *major* parties if I were you, Steven. We don't want to remind Mom and Dad what happened while they were in Mexico."

Steven shrugged casually. "Fine. So I'll just have a few friends over."

"No you won't. *I'm* having a few friends over!" Jessica cried.

"Sorry, shrimp," Steven said breezily. "You're out of luck."

"Nice meeting you, Melissa," Joe said, as he and Steven walked to the far side of the pool.

Jessica jumped out of her chair. "He's not going to get away with this!" she vowed. She grabbed Lila's arm. "Come on, Lila."

As Melissa watched Jessica and Steven arguing, she felt a sudden pang of wistfulness. She couldn't imagine getting annoyed with Andy over something as silly as a pool party—at least not now. They'd had their share of arguments over the years, but they couldn't afford to fight like Jessica and Steven. Not when they had so much at stake and only each other to depend on.

"Sorry about Jess and Steven," Elizabeth said. "They're going through one of those phases when they act like two-year-olds."

Amy giggled. "I can see you're going to have lots to write about for the social studies report, Melissa!"

"Andy and I have gone through times like that, too," Melissa said, watching Jessica and Steven thoughtfully. "I guess all brothers and sisters do."

Elizabeth sipped her lemonade. "Steven gets on my nerves, too, sometimes. But I know he'd do anything for me if I were in trouble."

"That's how Andy is. I suppose we're really more like best friends than brother and sister . . . especially now."

"Did your dad get back from overseas yet?" Elizabeth asked.

Melissa nodded. "A couple days ago." She hated lying to her new friends like this, but she didn't have any choice.

"I'm looking forward to meeting him for the project," Elizabeth continued.

Melissa felt a wave of panic. What was she going to do for a dad? Use Sam Hughes again? She'd have to send Mr. McCormick away on another imaginary trip to Europe.

She stood abruptly. "That reminds me. I should call Andy and tell him where I am. Can I use your phone?"

"Sure. It's in the kitchen," Elizabeth said. "I'll show you."

"That's OK. I remember."

When Andy answered the phone after several rings, he sounded breathless. "Hi," he said. "Where are you? I just walked in the door and I was worried."

"Sorry," Melissa said. "Elizabeth Wakefield invited me over to her house."

"Well, I wish you'd let me know first," Andy said accusingly.

"That's why I'm calling. Besides, I knew you'd be at basketball practice."

"OK," Andy said, his voice relaxing. "Sorry. We'll have to work out some sort of system so I always know where you are. Be home for dinner at six, OK?"

As Melissa hung up, she felt a twinge of resentment. It seemed strange to hear Andy talking to her like a parent.

The kitchen door opened and a tall man carrying a briefcase entered. "Hello," he said. "I'm Mr. Wakefield."

"I'm Melissa McCormick, a friend of Elizabeth's," Melissa said. "Nice to meet—"

Suddenly Jessica burst into the kitchen with Steven on her heels. "Dad, there's something I've *got* to discuss with you," she said urgently.

"Hey, I've got seniority, munchkin," Steven argued.

"Don't call me munchkin, Steven!" Jessica yelled. She turned to her father and smiled angelically. "Dad, I was wondering if you'd consider letting me have—"

"—a pool party," Steven interrupted. "Just a few of my friends. That Friday we have off from school."

"I thought of it first, Steven!" Jessica growled.

"Prove it in a court of law," Steven shouted back.

Mr. Wakefield crossed his arms over his chest. "You two are going to have to figure out a compromise on your own, or there won't be any pool party."

"But Dad—"

"End of story, Jessica," Mr. Wakefield cut in. He smiled apologetically at Melissa. "Sorry, Melissa," he said. "Just a little friendly family discussion. You know how those can be!"

"Oh, sure," Melissa said with an uneasy laugh. "My brother and I are the same way."

Melissa followed Jessica and Steven back outside. She was talking to Elizabeth when she turned around just in time to see Jessica and Lila push Steven into the pool.

Melissa wondered if she and Andy would ever have that kind of fun again.

Nine

◆

After school the following Monday, Melissa stopped by the Francos' front yard to check on Mr. Franco's roses. They were doing pretty well, she thought proudly. Maybe not as well as they would have if her mom had been taking care of them. But at least they were still alive and blooming.

She crossed the driveway into her own yard and took her key out of her backpack. Andy would still be at basketball practice today. He'd drawn up a careful schedule so they'd each know where the other would be twenty-four hours a day.

She and Andy were beginning to fall into a routine now. It wasn't perfect, and it certainly wasn't like other families, but Melissa had begun to think they might make things work, after all.

Melissa unlocked the door and headed to the

kitchen for a snack. To her surprise, Andy was sitting at the table, his head in his hands. On the table was a huge stack of bills, a sheet of paper covered with scribbled numbers, and a calculator.

"Andy!" Melissa cried. "What are you doing here? You're supposed to be at basketball practice."

"Not anymore." Andy looked up, rubbing his eyes. There were dark circles under them that Melissa hadn't noticed before.

"What do you mean, 'not anymore'?"

Andy shrugged. "I quit the team today."

"You *quit*?"

"Don't make a big deal out of it, Melissa," Andy said curtly. "I really don't want to talk about it."

Melissa dropped into a chair. "You *have* to talk about it. You're the best center Sweet Valley's ever had," she said, remembering Steven Wakefield's words. She nodded at the towering pile of bills on the table. "Does your quitting have anything to do with those?"

"It's nothing to worry about," Andy insisted. "But I've been doing some calculations, and the money's going faster than I thought it would. I've decided to take on some part-time work to help out with the bills a little. It's something I should have done a long time ago. Maybe if I had, Mom—"

"Don't say it," Melissa interrupted quietly.

"I've been thinking the same thing, Andy. If only I'd gotten a job baby-sitting or something to help earn extra money, or if I'd helped more around the house . . ."

"Well, there's no point in worrying about all that now, Lissa," Andy replied. "We can't sit around blaming ourselves. Mom wouldn't want us to, and besides, her illness had nothing to do with us."

Melissa thumbed through the pile of bills. There were so many of them, and for so much money! Some had OVERDUE written on them in big red letters. "We have to pay for water?" she asked numbly as she got to the bottom of the pile.

"Yep," Andy answered. "But at least we won't have to pay for our fruit and vegetables soon. I got a part-time job as a produce clerk at the supermarket, and Mr. O'Neal says I can take home all the produce we can eat."

"Couldn't you still stay on the team, Andy?" Melissa asked. "Maybe the coach would let you skip some practices. I mean, you *are* the star of the team."

Andy shook his head. "That wouldn't be fair to the other guys on the team. Besides, I've already picked up some other little jobs around the neighborhood. Mowing lawns, that sort of thing."

"I'm going to get a job, too," Melissa said firmly. She wasn't about to let her brother make such a big sacrifice without doing her fair share.

"Absolutely not," Andy told her. "Your job is to concentrate on your schoolwork. Which reminds me. How did you do on that science quiz today?"

Melissa looked away. She was hoping he'd forgotten about that. "OK," she answered.

Andy narrowed his eyes. "What does *OK* mean, exactly?"

"C plus," Melissa said.

Andy looked disappointed—exactly like her mom would have looked. "You've always gotten A's in science, Melissa," he said.

"But this was really a tough quiz, Andy," she said pleadingly. "No one did very well. And I guess . . ." she trailed off. The truth was that she couldn't concentrate on school anymore. It seemed so unimportant now.

"After dinner, I'll help you with your science homework," Andy offered.

"But I don't *need* help, Andy."

"And I think maybe you should limit your TV until your science grades improve," Andy added distractedly as he began to sort through the bills again.

"Andy!" Melissa snapped. "You're not my—" She stopped herself before she said the word "dad." "Are you sure I can't take one little job?" she asked softly. "I could wash some cars, or maybe—"

"No," Andy said firmly. "I can manage, Lissa."

Melissa heard the tension in his voice and sighed. "Well, the least I can do is start dinner," she said at last.

Andy looked up from his calculator and smiled. "Maybe I should have let you get a job," he joked. "It might have been safer for my stomach."

Melissa laughed, but inside she felt like crying. They'd already lost so much, and she hated to see Andy give up basketball, too.

"We still need a good sports story for the next *Sixers* issue," Elizabeth said. It was Wednesday afternoon, and Elizabeth, Amy, Julie Porter, and Sophia Rizzo were gathered in the Wakefields' family room to plan the next week's edition of the school paper.

Sophia shook her head. "There's not much going on right now, Elizabeth. We already did that big cover story on the girls basketball team last week."

Elizabeth glanced over at Steven, who was lying on the couch, scanning the television guide. "Steven," she said, "can you think of any good ideas for a sports story?"

"Whatever you do don't try to talk to my coach. He's been in a foul mood since the varsity basketball team lost their star center."

"You mean Andy McCormick?" Elizabeth asked in surprise.

"He quit on Monday," Steven said. "Everyone at school's talking about it."

"I wonder why he quit?" Elizabeth asked.

"He said he was burned out on playing," Steven answered. "But somehow I doubt that was the real reason. He sure seemed to love the game. And Joe Howell said he saw Andy working at the Shop and Save yesterday."

Elizabeth frowned. "You know, I've tried to get together a couple times with Melissa to work on our families project," she told the other girls. "But she seems to be avoiding it." Elizabeth paused. "Not that I can blame her, after what she's just been through."

"First she loses her mom, then her dad suddenly moves back after her parents have been separated for years," Amy said. "Poor Melissa. That's a lot to handle."

Elizabeth jumped up. "I'm going to go give her a call. We'll be done with the *Sixers* stuff soon, and maybe she'll want to come over."

A few minutes later, Elizabeth returned to the family room. "Melissa said she was trying out a recipe for chicken casserole and couldn't leave. I guess she has to do a lot more of the housework now."

"I wish there were some way we could help her," Julie said.

"I do too," Elizabeth said. "But my mom said to give her time. She needs time to feel sad, and that's not something you can rush. I guess we shouldn't push her too hard."

Jessica entered the living room, carrying a peanut butter sandwich in one hand and a ham sandwich in the other.

"My sister," Steven said, laughing. "She's such a dainty eater!"

Elizabeth and her friends laughed, but Jessica wasn't amused at all. "You're one to talk, Steven. You're the only garbage disposal in America that burps!" She sat in an easy chair. "Give me the channel changer. *Days of Turmoil* is already half over."

"I'm watching wrestling," Steven argued.

"Well *I'm* not watching a bunch of fat guys sweat all over each other," Jessica said, taking a bite out of a sandwich.

"Come on, gang," Elizabeth said. "Let's go upstairs. Looks like the Wakefield Civil War is starting up again, and we don't want to get caught in the crossfire."

Just as the four girls started toward the stairs, Jessica tossed her peanut butter sandwich at Steven and scored a direct hit.

"Not bad," Melissa murmured as she checked the oven for the fourth time that afternoon. The chicken casserole she'd made was Andy's favorite. She'd watched her mom make it many times, but she'd never realized how complicated it was until she'd tried to follow the recipe herself. Still, it had been worth the trouble. The casserole smelled wonderful.

Andy was going to be so surprised when he got home from work at the supermarket! He needed some cheering up—Melissa knew how much he already missed basketball. And yesterday he'd gotten a D in English, one of his favorite subjects.

Melissa went to the living room and lay down on the couch. She was very sleepy. When she'd finally gone to bed last night, she'd had a hard time falling asleep. But then, that was nothing new. She never slept well anymore.

She pulled her mom's afghan over her legs and closed her eyes. The chicken still had forty minutes to cook. She'd set the timer on the stove, so she knew it would wake her up.

It didn't take long for Melissa to fall into a heavy sleep. In her dreams, she was having a hard time breathing, and the air had turned thick and gray. Every time she took a breath, her lungs burned.

She awoke with a start to see that she hadn't been dreaming. The oven was on fire!

Ten

◇

"No!" Melissa shouted as she jumped off the couch and dashed into the kitchen.

If the fire was too bad, she knew she should leave and call the fire department from a neighbor's house. But she could tell that the oven itself wasn't on fire—not yet, anyway. It was the chicken that was burning. Smoke was pouring through the cracks of the oven door as flames flickered inside.

Melissa ran to the broom closet where her mother kept a small fire extinguisher. Suddenly she was grateful for her mother's repeated instructions on how to use it. She pulled out the pin in the handle. Then, stepping back carefully, she put on an oven mit and pulled open the oven door. She aimed the extinguisher at the flames and squeezed the handle. Seconds later the fire was out.

Melissa slumped into a chair, staring at the

horrible mess. The inside of the oven was black, and a coating of white foam from the extinguisher dripped down the sides. The chicken—her beautiful casserole—was a sooty lump.

Melissa picked up her mother's recipe card. "Bake at 350 for fifty minutes," it said in her careful, beautiful handwriting. What had Melissa done wrong? The timer still hadn't gone off. She'd set the oven for the right temperature. Melissa glanced at the stove settings. Suddenly she realized her mistake. The oven was set to broil, not bake!

"I am such an idiot," Melissa murmured as tears welled up in her eyes. She couldn't seem to concentrate on anything lately, not even a simple recipe.

"Melissa?" Andy called as he opened the front door. "I hope you're hungry, because Mr. O'Neal gave me a lifetime supply of ban—"

He stopped in mid-sentence as he entered the kitchen, his mouth half open in shock. Then he took one look at Melissa and regained his composure. He set down the bag of bananas he was carrying and peered into the oven. "Mmmm," he said, rubbing his hands together, "chicken charcoal. My favorite!"

Melissa sniffled. "I am so stupid, Andy. I wanted to surprise you because you've been working so hard, and I know how much you love Mom's casserole—"

"Hey," Andy said, coming over to give her a hug. "I had a craving for pizza tonight, anyway."

"We can't afford pizza."

"You have a better idea?"

Melissa forced herself to smile. "Bananas?"

Andy laughed. He got down on his knees and examined the oven more carefully. "Well, the good news is, I think it can be repaired. Unfortunately, I can't do it. We're going to have to call a repairman tomorrow."

"That's going to cost a lot of money, isn't it?" Melissa asked, dreading the answer.

"I guess so." Andy cast a quick glance at the pile of bills on the table. "And we're already barely making ends meet."

"I'm getting a job," Melissa said firmly. "And don't argue with me this time, Andy."

"This time I can't argue with you, kid. We need every penny we can get."

"I'm really sorry, Andy," Melissa said quietly.

Andy closed the oven door. "I always said you were a lousy cook," he said with a laugh. "Now what do you want on your pizza?"

"Anything but chicken," Melissa answered, but she wasn't laughing.

By the following day, Melissa was able to joke about the fire. "I guess I'm not cut out to be a chef," she told Elizabeth with a sheepish grin.

The two girls were in the library. At Elizabeth's suggestion, they'd had a quick lunch and gone straight to the library to work on their families project. Melissa was almost relieved that they were finally working on the project. She knew she couldn't avoid it forever. And to her relief, things had been going smoothly so far. She'd had a story ready for every question Elizabeth asked about her family.

"I'm not much of a cook, either," Elizabeth admitted when Melissa finished her tale of the charcoal chicken. "Don't feel bad, Melissa."

"I did feel bad," Melissa said. "Terrible, in fact. But at least I can laugh about it today. And anyway, I'd rather be a mystery writer than a chef."

"I *love* mysteries!" Elizabeth exclaimed. "Especially Amanda Howard. I just finished *The Case of the Missing Magician*."

"I'd love to read that," Melissa said. "Amanda Howard's one of my favorite authors."

"You can borrow the book," Elizabeth said. She leaned back in her chair and smiled. "You know, we have a lot in common. We both like to write, we both love Amanda Howard, we both have older brothers who play—" She paused. "Oh, I forgot. Steven told me that Andy quit the team."

Melissa began doodling with her pencil on the cover of her notebook. "He was tired of playing," she said casually. She glanced over at Elizabeth's notes. "So," she said brightly, "where were we on the project?"

"Let's see," Elizabeth said. She checked the list of questions she'd compiled. "We just finished my dad, and we were going to talk some more ·about yours."

Melissa looked past Elizabeth out the window. "There's not much to say, really," she said evasively. "He's just a dad, like any dad."

Elizabeth shook her head and laughed. "You'll have to do better than that, Melissa. I don't think Mrs. Arnette will be too impressed with my research if I just say 'Mr. McCormick is a typical dad'! Of course, when I meet him, I can ask him more questions myself."

Melissa looked down at her notebook. "Sure," she said quietly. "You'll really like him. He travels a lot, though, Elizabeth. He might be in Europe soon. It'd be a shame if you didn't get to meet him."

"I thought he just got back from Europe," Elizabeth said.

"Well, he did," Melissa responded carefully. "But they might need him back."

"What does he do for a living?" Elizabeth asked, crossing off a question on her list.

"Music," Melissa said, trying to remember exactly what Andy had told Mr. and Mrs. Franco. "He sells music. You know, to orchestras and bands and things."

"That must be an interesting job," Elizabeth said.

"Oh, it is," Melissa said quickly. She thought it was a good idea to expand the lie a bit, to make it more believable. "He's always bringing us interesting things home. Last Christmas he brought me a cuckoo clock from Germany."

"I thought you said you hadn't seen your dad in years," Elizabeth said.

Melissa felt her stomach drop. "I meant, hardly ever," she said unsteadily. "He usually comes home for big holidays."

"Oh," Elizabeth said uncertainly.

Melissa shoved her chair back abruptly. "Could we do this another time, Elizabeth?" she asked. "I just remembered something I have to do."

"What?"

"Some, uh, some homework I forgot to finish," Melissa lied.

She turned and ran for the door before Elizabeth could ask any other questions—questions Melissa knew she wouldn't have the answers for.

The following Monday, Melissa started a paper route. She'd been surprised at how easy it was for her to get the job. She'd been even more surprised at how sore she was by the time she finished delivering all her papers. Every muscle in her body hurt. Her bag of newspapers seemed to weigh at least a ton.

Melissa tossed her newspaper bag on the floor and sank onto the couch. She glanced at her watch. She knew Andy wouldn't be home for another couple of hours, so she decided to take a nap.

Just as she closed her eyes, Melissa heard someone knocking at the door. With a groan, she forced herself off the couch. She peeked through the peephole in the door.

"Elizabeth!" Melissa exclaimed as she unlocked the door and opened it.

"I hope you're not in the middle of dinner," Elizabeth said. "I thought I'd drop off this book."

"The Amanda Howard mystery!" Melissa said excitedly as Elizabeth stepped inside. "Thanks, Elizabeth." She pointed to a chair. "Have a seat."

"I can only stay a minute," Elizabeth said. "We'll be having dinner soon." She glanced around the room. "Is your dad home yet?"

"My dad?" Melissa echoed warily. "Oh no. He's working late tonight. So's Andy."

"I thought Steven told me Andy worked at the grocery store. Does he have a paper route, too?" Elizabeth asked. She pointed to the newspaper bag lying on the floor.

"Yes," Melissa lied. As soon as she'd answered, she regretted it. What if Elizabeth saw her delivering papers someday? How could Melissa explain that?

"I mean," Melissa corrected herself, "he *used* to have a paper route. Now I do it."

Elizabeth raised her brows. "I'll bet that's a lot of work."

"It is." Melissa nodded. "More than I thought it would be." She shrugged. "The truth is, I just started the route today. And every single muscle in my body aches!"

Elizabeth smiled sympathetically. "It'll be nice to have the extra money though."

Melissa sighed. "We do have a lot of bills piling up," she said without thinking.

Suddenly she panicked. How could she have been so stupid to mention the bills? She felt her face begin to flush again.

"Melissa? Is anything wrong?" Elizabeth asked. "Anything you want to talk about?"

Melissa looked at Elizabeth's sympathetic expression, and all at once she didn't care if she was supposed to be keeping secrets. She didn't have the strength to lie anymore. She wanted a friend, someone whom she could confide in.

"Elizabeth," she began, her voice shaking, "I've been lying to you. To everybody."

"It's OK, Melissa," Elizabeth said. "You're not exactly the first person to ever tell a lie."

"But this is a big one," Melissa insisted. "And I don't know how much longer we can keep it going."

"Is this about your dad?"

"How did you know?"

"You seemed so uneasy talking about him,"

Elizabeth said. "Are you having problems getting along?"

"No," Melissa said dryly. "We get along just fine. Especially since we haven't seen each other in years."

"You mean—"

"I have no idea where my dad is, Elizabeth. He could be at the North Pole, for all I know. Andy and I just pretended he was coming home because the department of social services would split us up if we didn't have adult supervision." She smiled. "Andy was very ingenious. He got a friend of his to call everyone, pretending to be our dad."

"So that's why you and Andy have started working," Elizabeth said.

"The money's running out a lot faster than we thought it would," Melissa confirmed. "And I'm so worried about Andy. When he's not working at the supermarket, he's doing odd jobs around the neighborhood. And he tries so hard to put up a brave front so I won't worry. But I can tell he's afraid everything's going to fall apart."

Melissa took a deep breath. She felt better telling Elizabeth the truth, even if it would make Andy angry. She was sure she could trust Elizabeth.

Elizabeth shook her head. "I can't believe all you've been through, Melissa. I'm not sure I could be as strong as you and Andy have been."

"Do you think we're doing the right thing?"

Elizabeth hesitated. "I don't know. But I do know if someone tried to separate me from Jessica, I'd do everything in my power to keep it from happening."

Melissa felt as if a great weight had been lifted off her shoulders. "Thanks, Elizabeth," she said. "That makes me feel a lot better."

"But don't you think you should tell *someone*?" Elizabeth asked. "A teacher at school, maybe?"

"No!" Melissa answered, nearly shouting. "You have to promise me you won't tell a soul, Elizabeth. If anyone finds out, Andy and I could end up in foster homes. And if I were separated from him now, I don't know what I'd do. I don't think I could stand it."

Elizabeth nodded. "I promise, Melissa," she said, but Melissa saw doubt in her eyes.

Eleven

◇

After school the next day, Elizabeth was passing through the family room when she noticed Jessica measuring the couch with a yardstick.

"What are you doing, Jessica?" she asked.

"Sixty-six inches," Jessica said to herself. "That's thirty-three for him and thirty-three for me." She motioned to Elizabeth. "Could you help me with this masking tape? I need to mark the halfway point."

"Do you mind if I ask why?"

"Why do you think?" Jessica said as though it were obvious. "Last night Steven and I were on the couch watching TV, and he insisted on putting his disgusting, smelly feet on my side of the couch."

Elizabeth groaned. "So you're going to divide the couch in half with masking tape? Don't you think Mom may have something to say about this when she gets home from work?"

"It comes right off, Elizabeth," Jessica snapped. She peeled off a long strip of tape and applied it to the center cushion.

"Jessica," Elizabeth said seriously, "I just don't understand why you and Steven are at each other's throats lately."

Jessica let out an exasperated sigh. "You mean to tell me that Steven doesn't get on *your* nerves? I guess I'm just not as tolerant as you, Saint Elizabeth."

"Of course he gets on my nerves," Elizabeth said. "That's what brothers are supposed to do. It's their job."

Jessica went back to her masking tape.

"Come on Jess, I'm serious," Elizabeth continued. "What is masking tape on the couch really going to solve?"

Jessica shrugged. "It's the *principle* of the thing, Lizzie."

"What principle?"

"I'm not sure exactly," Jessica said. "Can I get back to you on that one?"

"See?" Elizabeth said, exasperated. "You don't even remember what this feud is about!"

"That doesn't mean I'm going to be the one who caves in," Jessica said. She applied one last piece of tape and paused to admire her handiwork. "Steven should apologize to me, Elizabeth."

Elizabeth rolled her eyes toward the ceiling. "Fine. Have it your way, Jess. And while you're at it, why don't you just divide the whole house in half?"

Jessica's eyes lit up. "Great idea, Lizzie! Why didn't I think of that?"

As Elizabeth turned to leave, she saw Jessica on her hands and knees, carefully measuring the coffee table.

When Melissa got home from her paper route, she found Elizabeth sitting on the front steps of the McCormicks' house.

"Hi, Elizabeth," Melissa said as she sank onto the steps. "Want a paper? I have a few extra today."

"Actually, I stopped by to see if you wanted some help fixing dinner. Not that I'm much of a cook. But at least I've never charbroiled an oven!"

Melissa laughed. "I can use all the help I can get." She pulled her key out of her jeans pocket.

"To tell you the truth, I wanted a place to hide out for a while," Elizabeth admitted as she followed Melissa inside the house. "Jessica and Steven are at it again."

"In a way they're lucky. Andy and I don't see

each other enough these days to fight, even if we wanted to."

"Did you tell him?" Elizabeth asked. "That you told me, I mean?"

Melissa shook her head. "He came home late last night, and he was really tired. I just didn't want to bring it up."

"I understand," Elizabeth said. "You know, you look kind of tired yourself, Melissa."

"Not as tired as Andy looks," Melissa responded. She tossed her newspaper bag onto a chair with a sigh. "Boy, this place is a mess, isn't it? I haven't had a lot of time to clean up lately. I guess it shows, huh?"

"Tell you what," Elizabeth said. "I'll give you a hand cleaning up before we start dinner, OK?"

Melissa smiled at her new friend gratefully. "What do you get out of the deal?"

"I get a vacation from Jessica and Steven."

For the next hour, the girls vacuumed and dusted and organized the house. When they were done with the living room, they worked on Melissa's bedroom. Then they moved on to Andy's.

Elizabeth was pushing the vacuum down the hallway when she paused in front of Mrs. McCormick's bedroom. "How about this room?" she asked.

Melissa hesitated. She hadn't been back in her

mom's room since the night she'd slept there. "That's my mom's bedroom," she said quietly.

"Oh, I'm sorry, Melissa," Elizabeth said quickly. She started to move down the hall, but Melissa stopped her.

"Wait, Elizabeth," she whispered. "I really should go in there and clean up. I've only gone in once since . . . I'd feel better if you were with me."

Elizabeth nodded. Melissa eased the door open, and once again, the sweet scent of her mom's perfume made her eyes fill with tears. Melissa took a deep breath. "I should make the bed," she stated flatly. "And maybe you could—I don't know—straighten up a little?"

The girls worked silently for a few minutes. As Elizabeth folded some clothes that were lying on a chair, she pointed to a small framed photo on Mrs. McCormick's dresser. "Is that your mom?" she asked softly.

Melissa nodded. "And my dad. Right after they got married. They were crazy about each other then."

"She was really beautiful," Elizabeth said, examining the photo more carefully. "You look like her."

"Do you really think so?" Melissa asked.

"A lot."

The thought made Melissa smile. As she

leaned down to tuck in a sheet, her hand brushed something underneath the bed. She kneeled down to see what it was and discovered a thick pile of envelopes, bound together by a red ribbon.

"I wonder what these are?" she said.

"What?"

"Letters." Melissa hesitated. *These belong to Mom*, she told herself. *They're not my business.*

But just then a return address on the top envelope caught her eye. "J. McCormick," she read quietly. She checked the postmark dates and looked up at Elizabeth. "These are from my dad, Elizabeth! I had no idea he'd written my mom so many times. After the first few letters, I thought he'd stopped writing."

Elizabeth sat down on the corner of the bed. "She never told you he kept writing?"

Melissa shook her head. "Once my parents separated, I think she wanted to get on with her life."

"Why did they separate?" Elizabeth asked gently. "Do you know?"

"All I know is near the end it seemed like they were fighting all the time," Melissa answered, fingering the red bow on the sheaf of letters. "I'm not exactly sure what finally drove them apart. But I know it had something to do with my dad's wanting to be a musician." She smiled. "You should have heard him play the guitar, Elizabeth. He had the most incredible voice. And he wrote beautiful songs. But he never made it big. He was always holding down these part-time jobs so he could play in clubs at night."

"It sounds sort of romantic," Elizabeth said.

"Yeah," Melissa said, "but I guess my mom didn't think so. She wanted my dad to settle down and give up on music, and my dad just couldn't." She looked down at the letters. "Do you think he might have mentioned me in any of these?"

Elizabeth seemed to read her mind. "I think your mom would understand if you wanted to read some of those letters."

"I just want to know if he ever asked about Andy or me," Melissa said, her voice barely a whisper. "That's all."

Elizabeth nodded. "I'll help, if you like."

Carefully Melissa untied the ribbon. She handed half the letters to Elizabeth and took half for herself.

"These postmarks are from all over the country," Elizabeth remarked.

"It looks like the last one came about a year ago," Melissa said. "I wonder if he even knows where we live now." She removed one of the letters and unfolded it. It was written on lined notebook paper in her dad's messy scrawl.

Melissa read the letter silently, her eyes scanning the lines for her name or Andy's. Near the bottom of the page, she found them. *Please, Jan,* the letter said, *please consider letting us try to make things work one last time. Don't we owe it to the kids? There aren't any words to tell you how much I miss Melissa and Andy.*

"He wanted to get back together with my mom, Elizabeth!" Melissa said in amazement. "And he really missed us."

"He said the same things in this letter," Elizabeth confirmed. "And he asked why your mom kept sending back the money he mailed to her."

"He sent Mom money?" Melissa exclaimed. "She never told us that."

"Maybe she was too proud to keep it," Elizabeth suggested.

For the next half hour, the girls read through the letters, one by one. Whether the postmark was from California or Maine, the message was always the same.

When they were all done, Melissa stacked the letters together and tied them with the bow. "I felt a little guilty reading these," she told Elizabeth, "but now I'm glad I did. It helps me to understand that my dad really did love Andy and me. I guess Dad and Mom were just too different to work things out."

"Melissa," Elizabeth said excitedly. "I have an idea. Suppose we try to write your dad and tell him everything that's happened? Who knows? Maybe he'd come to Sweet Valley so you could all be together."

Melissa shook her head grimly. "Write to him *where?* His last letter was from a hotel in Houston, Texas, and he wrote that a year ago."

"But we could at least try—"

"No," Melissa said firmly. "I don't want to try. What if he doesn't respond? I just couldn't bear it." She pushed the pile of letters under the bed where she'd found them. "Besides, I found out just now what I needed to know." She stood and stretched. "And that's better than nothing, which is what I had before."

"Great dinner," Andy commented as he finished a second helping of tuna casserole that evening.

"Elizabeth helped me," Melissa admitted. "I can't take all the credit. She helped me clean up around here, too."

"I noticed," Andy said appreciatively. "It almost looks like a real house again."

"We cleaned up Mom's room, too," Melissa said quickly. She stood up and began to clear the table.

"You went in Mom's room?"

"Somebody had to eventually."

Andy tossed his napkin onto the table. "You're right," he said firmly. "Thanks for doing it, Lissa."

Melissa stared at her plate. "Andy, I told Elizabeth about us."

"You *what?*" Andy shouted.

"We can trust her, Andy. She promised not to tell."

"That's not good enough, Melissa. We can't trust anyone!"

Andy rubbed his eyes with his hand, and Melissa thought she'd never seen him look so tired. "Andy, you've got to believe me. Elizabeth knows what could happen to us if she told our secret. And all she wants to do is help." She touched his shoulder. "She told me that if she were in our position, she'd probably have done the same thing."

Andy let out a deep, long sigh. "I hope you're right, Melissa."

"I am."

"No one else, though," he warned. "Promise me you won't tell anyone else."

"I won't tell another soul." Melissa laid the dishes in the sink. "There's something else, Andy."

Andy glared at her. "That's not enough for one night?"

Melissa sat down across from him. "I found some letters in Mom's room. Lots of them. They were all from Dad—"

Andy let out a loud groan.

"Listen to me, Andy!" Melissa pleaded. "He wanted Mom to take him back. He asked her again and again. And he even sent her money."

"You actually believe those letters?" Andy asked bitterly.

"Why shouldn't I?"

Andy pushed back his chair and stood. "Have you ever heard the expression, 'actions speak louder than words'? Well, Dad was great with words, Melissa. He loved to make promises. He just wasn't so hot on the follow-through."

Without another word, he headed for his room and slammed the door.

The sound echoed in the still house. With a sigh, Melissa began to wash the dishes. "I tried, Dad," she whispered, to no one in particular.

Twelve

◇

"Melissa, meet Sam Hughes."

Melissa dropped her newspaper bag on the floor and stared from Andy's face to Sam's and back again. It was Thursday afternoon, and she hadn't expected Andy to be back from work for another few hours.

"What's going on?" Melissa asked. "Why aren't you at work, Andy?"

Sam propped his feet up on the coffee table. "Big brother had a little run-in with the principal. Right, Andy?" He consulted his watch, a large expensive-looking one with diamonds on the face. "Ol' lady Hollingsworth should be calling Daddy any minute."

"Daddy?"

"Yours truly. Aren't you glad to see me, kid?"

"Knock it off, Hughes," Andy warned with a fierce glare.

Melissa turned to Andy. "Did you get in some kind of trouble at school, Andy?"

"I've missed a few days lately," Andy admitted. "So I could pick up some more odd jobs. Ms. Hollingsworth called me into the office today. She said she wanted to meet with my father to discuss my absences. I told her he was leaving town on business soon, but she could probably reach him this afternoon." He grimaced. "Sam agreed to help out."

"Free of charge, no less," Sam added. "Out of the goodness of my heart."

Melissa cast a sidelong glance at Sam. She didn't like him, and she had a feeling they couldn't trust him.

The phone rang, and Andy reached for it.

"Let Daddy get it," Sam said, grabbing the receiver. He cleared his throat and winked at Melissa. "Jack McCormick," he answered gruffly.

Melissa looked at Andy, who shrugged helplessly.

"I'm very sorry to hear that," Sam said. "What did you say your name was again? Wendy? Lovely name."

Sam rolled his eyes as he listened to Ms. Hollingsworth's reply. "Well, boys will be boys, Wendy. May I call you Wendy? I promise you, I'm going to have a long talk with Andy and straighten that boy right out."

There was another long pause. "Yes, it's true, he's been through a lot," Sam said. "Thank you. Yes, yes, the loss came as quite a shock." Sam covered his mouth to keep from laughing. "Yes, I certainly will. And thank you for bringing this to my attention, Wendy."

Sam hung up the phone and began to applaud his performance. "How do you like that?" he shouted. "*Wendy!* That witch Hollingsworth and I are on a first-name basis now."

Andy stood abruptly. "Well, thanks, Sam," he said uneasily, avoiding Melissa's eyes. "I really appreciate your help."

"Hey, no sweat," Sam replied. "I'll think of a way you can return the favor." He walked to the door, then paused. "See ya, kids," he said with a smile that sent shivers down Melissa's spine.

She rushed over and slammed the door shut behind him. "I don't trust that guy," she told Andy.

"Neither do I," Andy said tensely. "But what choice did I have?"

"You were worried about me telling Elizabeth our secret," Melissa said. "I think it's Sam we've got to worry about."

"I know," Andy said wearily. "We'll just have to keep our fingers crossed."

"What did he mean when he said you could return the favor?"

Andy threw up his hands. "Your guess is as good as mine, Lissa."

On Friday night, Melissa made a special dinner. Andy looked like he was losing weight, and she'd decided that it was her job to fatten him up. She made her mom's chicken casserole again, and this time it turned out perfectly. She even put a vase of Mr. Franco's roses on the table as a centerpiece.

But when Andy came home from work, he didn't even notice her efforts. Instead he headed straight for his room without even saying hello.

Melissa followed him and knocked on his bedroom door. "Andy?" she called. "Are you all right?"

"I'll be out in a while," he answered strangely. "I just want to take a little rest."

"But I made us a gourmet dinner," Melissa protested. "It may even be edible this time."

When he didn't answer, Melissa inched the door open. Andy was lying on his bed, his forearm over his eyes. There were tears streaming down his cheeks.

"Andy?" Melissa said softly. She walked over and sat down on his bed.

"I'm OK, really," he said. "Please go, Melissa."

Melissa didn't move. It was the first time she'd witnessed Andy crying since the day her mom had died. Seeing him this way scared her. But right now, Andy needed her to be strong.

"Andy," she pressed, "you've got to tell me what's wrong. I'm not leaving until you do."

Andy sat up and brushed away his tears impatiently. "I'm sorry, Lissa. I guess it all just kind of caught up with me for a moment there. I haven't been sleeping real well—"

"Me either."

"And I just felt sort of overwhelmed." He smiled, but it wasn't his usual easygoing smile. There was real fear in his dark green eyes. "Anyway, it's all over now."

Melissa shook her head. There was something else going on, and she was going to get to the bottom of it. "Andy," she said softly. "You don't always have to be the strong one, you know. It helps me if I can take care of you, too."

"I'm not really strong, Lissa," Andy said flatly. "I'm just a good actor."

"You had me fooled," Melissa whispered.

"Too bad I couldn't fool myself."

Melissa squeezed his hand. "You've got to tell me what's bothering you, Andy. I know there's more. Does this have anything to do with Sam?"

Andy looked away. "You were right about him, OK?"

"What do you mean?"

"He wants me to do something for him. Something illegal. And if I don't do it, he's threatening to tell social services about us." He shook his head sadly. "I wanted to make things work so badly, Lissa. I promised you. And now I'm as bad as Dad ever was."

Melissa gave him a long hug. "Hey. I couldn't ask for a better brother. A *neater* brother, maybe," she added, pointing at the pile of clothes on his floor. "But not a better one." She paused. "What exactly does Sam want you to do?"

"It's not important. I'm going to try to find a way to get out of it, though, Melissa. Trust me."

"I *do* trust you."

"Then that's the end of the subject. Except—" Andy paused. "There's something I wanted to tell you, Melissa."

"What?"

"I read those letters you told me about. The ones in Mom's room."

"And?"

"And maybe you were right about Dad. Maybe it was more complicated than I thought." He smiled grimly. "I'm starting to understand just how complicated things can get sometimes."

"I'm glad you read them, Andy. It makes things easier, doesn't it?"

"Yeah. It does." Andy got off the bed and stretched. "So how about some of that gourmet dinner? Suddenly I'm starving."

Melissa hesitated. "Andy?"

"Yes?"

"Just promise me you won't do anything you'll be sorry for later, OK?"

Andy nodded. But the look in his eyes made Melissa fear this might be one promise he wouldn't be able to keep.

Sam was all Melissa could think about during social studies class on Monday. The more she thought about it, the more she felt certain that things were going to fall apart, and Sam would be to blame. As long as he knew their secret, they were in danger.

Mrs. Arnette droned on about the traits of a happy family, listing them one by one on the blackboard.

Melissa glanced at the list indifferently. Several people had suggested "honesty." Others had said "loyalty" or "love." Mrs. Arnette had added "sharing" and "cooperation" to the list.

"A happy family is one without any brothers," Jessica had suggested.

Mrs. Arnette left that one off the list.

As she listened to the rest of the class talk about their families, Melissa wondered about her own. Did she and Andy even count as a real family? They had all the traits listed on Mrs. Arnette's blackboard. But Melissa couldn't say they were exactly happy.

"One last thing, class," Mrs. Arnette said when the bell rang. "I have a little surprise for you. The next unit will be on pioneer families, and it won't be taught by me."

There was a scattering of applause, until Mrs. Arnette shot a warning glance at the class. "You are going to have a student teacher for two weeks."

"All right!" Jessica exclaimed. "A two-week vacation!"

"That's where you're wrong, Jessica," Mrs. Arnette said. "I expect you all to work even harder than usual while Ms. Shepard is with us."

Melissa smiled grimly. Harder than usual? She could barely get any schoolwork done now.

When Mrs. Arnette finally dismissed them, Melissa dashed out of the room and ran to the girls' rest room. For some reason, she felt like crying, and she wanted some privacy. She'd just locked herself into a stall when she heard Elizabeth call her name.

"Melissa?" she yelled. "Are you OK?"

Melissa fought back her tears and opened the door. "Hi, Elizabeth," she said, sniffling.

Elizabeth led her to the far corner of the rest room. "What's wrong, Melissa?" she asked.

"I guess all that family stuff just bored me to tears," Melissa joked lamely.

"You can tell me, Melissa," Elizabeth urged.

Melissa waited until the rest room was empty. "I shouldn't be telling you this," she said. "Andy would kill me if he found out."

"I promise not to tell," Elizabeth vowed.

Melissa glanced at the door to make sure no one was coming. "It's Andy. He asked this guy Sam to pretend to be my dad and talk to the principal about Andy's absences. Now Sam is trying to blackmail Andy."

"Blackmail?" Elizabeth repeated, her eyes wide.

"He wants Andy to help him do something illegal, or he's going to tell social services about us," Melissa explained, gulping back a sob. "But that's all Andy will tell me. I'm scared to death he'll do whatever Sam wants, Elizabeth. Andy would do anything to keep us together."

"Could Sam have been bluffing?" Elizabeth asked, a worried look on her face.

Melissa shook her head. "You haven't met Sam."

Elizabeth leaned against a sink, deep in thought. "It might be time for you to tell someone, Melissa," she suggested gently. "A teacher, a counselor. You could even talk to my parents, if you like—"

"No!" Melissa shouted. Her voice echoed against the tile walls. "I can't take that risk, Elizabeth. I just can't!"

"Is that for your families project?" Elizabeth asked Jessica as she poured herself a glass of milk Wednesday afternoon.

"Nope," Jessica replied, looking up from her drawing. "I'm already done with that."

"You're *done*?" Elizabeth repeated. She and Melissa had barely started theirs.

Jessica grinned. "You don't actually mean to tell me I've finished a homework assignment *before* you?" She shook her head regretfully. "This is really going to be bad for my image, Lizzie."

"Melissa and I are having a hard time getting our schedules coordinated," Elizabeth explained. She sat down at the table. "Jess? What would you do if someone told you a secret and you promised not to tell a soul about it," Elizabeth began. "But then you started to think that you could help that person more if you told the secret to other people who would know what to do?"

Jessica dropped her pen. "Sounds juicy!" she exclaimed. "Who is this about, Lizzie? I can't wait to hear."

"This is just hypothetical, Jessica."

"Hypo-*what*?"

"There isn't any secret. We're just supposing."

"Oh." Jessica looked disappointed. "Well, then, I *suppose* what I'd do is tell the secret, if it would help the person." She shrugged. "Of course, I'd probably tell the secret anyway. You know me."

Elizabeth smiled at her twin and shook her head. "So what are you making?" she asked.

"Well, the tape idea didn't work out so well," Jessica admitted. "You were right. Mom wasn't too thrilled about having masking tape all over the family room. So I came up with another idea. Something that will prove to Mom and Dad that I am naturally superior to Steven in every way. Then they'll have to let me have my pool party."

Elizabeth rolled her eyes. "I can't wait to hear."

Jessica held up a piece of paper so Elizabeth could read it.

"Jerk-o-meter?" Elizabeth read.

"It rhymes with *thermometer*, Lizzie," Jessica said impatiently. "From now on, I'm keeping score. Every time Steven does something obnoxious, I write it down on this sheet of paper. He gets more points, depending on how annoying he is."

"Brilliant plan, Jess."

"Thanks," Jessica said proudly. "Say he burps, for example. A soft burp gets one point. A medium gets two. An eardrum-buster gets three points."

"Very scientific."

"You bet," Jessica agreed. "I still haven't assigned a point value to phone-hogging, though. After all, it's a more serious offense. What do you think?"

Elizabeth shoved back her chair. It was obvious Jessica wasn't going to be any help solving her dilemma about Melissa.

"How about ten points?" Jessica asked. "That seems reasonable. After all, I want to do what's right."

Elizabeth gave a resigned nod. "I know what you mean, Jess," she said. "So do I."

Thirteen

◇

Melissa stared at the pile of dishes in the sink and groaned. "Well, you're not going to clean yourselves," she muttered. "So I guess I'm elected."

It was Friday night, and she'd just eaten another dinner alone. Andy was working late at the supermarket again. They had another big electricity bill, and he was hoping his overtime pay would be enough to cover it.

But overdue bills weren't their worst problem. Melissa sighed, wondering for the hundredth time what they were going to do about Sam. Andy hadn't mentioned him again, and whenever she tried to bring him up, Andy avoided her questions.

Melissa filled the sink with hot soapy water. She wondered how much longer they would have hot water—or lights, for that matter. That afternoon, she'd come home from her paper route to hear the phone ringing. She'd hoped it was Elizabeth or Andy, but it was someone from the collections department at the electric company. "Please give us a little more time," Melissa had pleaded, but the collections lady was firm. Andy and Melissa had until next Friday to come up with their overdue payment. The electric company had already extended them extra time, the woman said. Did Melissa expect the company to survive on promises?

Melissa picked up a glass and began to sponge it distractedly. Outside the window, Mr. Franco's roses seemed to glow in the pale moonlight. They were doing beautifully. Caring for the roses seemed to be the one thing she'd been able to do well lately. Mr. Franco was going to be so pleased when he returned.

Suddenly a fleeting shadow passed over the roses. Melissa leaned over the sink to peer out the window, but the yard appeared to be empty. "Great," she said to herself. "Now I'm starting to see things."

But a second later, she knew it wasn't her imagination. Three figures dressed in black were tiptoeing along the side of the Francos' house. Somebody was trying to break in!

Melissa dropped her sponge and ran to the telephone. With trembling fingers, she dialed 911. "Hello?" she said. "My name is Melissa McCormick, and I'm calling to report a burglary. Not my house, the house next door. I just saw the guys."

She gave the police dispatcher the Francos' address and promised to stay in the house until the police arrived to investigate.

After she hung up the phone, she checked all the doors and windows to make sure they were locked. Then she turned off the kitchen light and peeked out the window again. The burglars had broken into one of the Francos' bedroom windows. She could see the bent screen lying on the ground.

"Poor Mr. and Mrs. Franco," she murmured, thinking of their pretty home. It wasn't fair that something like this should happen to such nice people.

She went to the living room and peered through the curtains. "Hurry," she said urgently. If the police didn't get there soon, the burglars would get away. The Francos didn't own much, but there was that beautiful silver tea set that Mrs. Franco was so proud of.

Just then two patrol cars eased down the street, their lights off so that the burglars wouldn't know they were approaching. Melissa felt a surge of relief.

Melissa watched as the police jumped from their cars and quickly surrounded the house. Then, with their guns drawn, two officers, a man and a woman, broke down the Francos' front door. Melissa heard muffled shouts. Seconds later, the lights went on in the house, and the woman officer stepped back onto the porch. "All clear," she called to the other police outside.

Melissa sighed with relief. She had to admit she felt a little proud. Wait until Andy found out that she'd helped capture three burglars! Too bad he'd had to work and miss all the excitement.

She unlocked the front door and stepped onto the porch, knowing it was safe, now that the three men had been captured. Other neighbors were standing in the street talking quietly.

Melissa watched as the burglars emerged. Their heads were hung low, and their hands were handcuffed behind their backs. One by one, they ducked into the backseat of a waiting police car. Melissa craned her neck to get a better view. They looked smaller and younger than she'd imagined, but their faces were obscured in the darkness.

The police car rolled past the McCormicks' front yard, as neighbors pointed and gawked. Melissa couldn't help staring at the car, too, hoping for a glimpse of the burglars.

Suddenly her heart stood still.

Peering out of the back window was a young man, his eyes glimmering with tears.

It was Andy.

"You have now scored two hundred and seventy-three points on the Jerk-o-meter," Jessica announced to Steven that night.

"Great," Steven replied indifferently. "What's my prize?"

"Could you two bicker somewhere else?" Elizabeth said as she entered the family room. "I need to talk to Mom and Dad alone."

Mr. Wakefield set his newspaper aside. "What is it, Elizabeth? You look upset."

Elizabeth sat down on the couch next to her father.

"Don't you two have some homework to do?" Mr. Wakefield asked Jessica and Steven.

"It's Friday night, Dad," Jessica pointed out.

"Good. You'll get a head start," Mrs. Wakefield replied, nodding toward the door.

When they'd gone upstairs, Mr. Wakefield turned to Elizabeth. "What's wrong, honey?" he asked.

"It's not me," she said slowly. "It's Melissa McCormick, a friend of mine." She clasped and unclasped her hands. *Was she doing the right thing?*

"What's the problem?" Mrs. Wakefield asked with concern.

Elizabeth hesitated. She had to tell someone about Melissa and Andy if it might help, didn't she? She couldn't just sit back and let them fall apart.

Just then the phone rang. "Elizabeth?" Jessica called from the upstairs hallway. "It's Melissa. She sounds really upset."

Could she already be too late? "I'll be right back," Elizabeth told her parents as she dashed for the telephone.

As Elizabeth listened in horror, Melissa told her the story of Andy's arrest. Her words were interrupted by huge sobs.

"I did it, Elizabeth," she cried. "I had my own brother arrested! It's my fault Andy's in jail right now!"

"It's not your fault, Melissa," Elizabeth insisted. But secretly, she was feeling responsible, too. Why hadn't she done something sooner? If she'd gone to her parents before, this whole nightmare might have been prevented.

"Listen," Elizabeth said. "I want you to stay right there, OK? I'm going to come over with my dad. He's a lawyer, and I think he can help Andy."

"Thank you, Elizabeth," Melissa said, her voice quaking. "I don't know what I'd do if I didn't have you for a friend right now."

Elizabeth hung up the phone with tears in her eyes. *Maybe if I'd been a better friend,* she thought bitterly, *none of this would have happened.*

"What happened?" Jessica demanded as soon as Mr. Wakefield and Elizabeth walked through the front door late that night.

"Is Andy still in jail?" Steven asked, rushing over.

"Give us a minute to sit down," Mr. Wakefield said wearily. "It's been a long night."

The family gathered in the living room. "I posted bail for Andy," Mr. Wakefield explained. "That means I gave money to the court as a guarantee that he would show up when his trial starts."

"So that means he's free?" Jessica asked.

Elizabeth shook her head. "Not exactly," she said, wiping away a tear.

"Andy and Melissa are being placed in temporary foster homes," Mr. Wakefield said.

"Oh, no," Mrs. Wakefield cried. "Couldn't we have taken them in, Ned?"

"I tried," Mr. Wakefield answered. "But the judge insisted on placing them in foster homes that are certified by the state. It would take weeks before we could get cleared to take the kids in, and by then Andy should already have been to trial."

"But why did they have to separate them?" Elizabeth sobbed. "Haven't they been through enough already?"

"They just didn't have a foster home available that could take them both," Mr. Wakefield explained with a sigh.

"I don't get it," Steven said. "Andy always seemed like such a good guy. Why would he get involved in something like this?"

"He didn't think he had a choice," Elizabeth

answered. She recounted Andy and Melissa's story while Jessica and Steven listened in shocked silence.

"If only I'd gone to Mom and Dad sooner," Elizabeth finished. "Maybe none of this would have happened."

"So that's why you were asking me about keeping secrets!" Jessica said. She looked at Elizabeth thoughtfully. "I wish I could have helped you more, Lizzie. But I guess I was too busy fighting with Steven to be much use." She shook her head. "I'm sorry. What a jerk I've been."

Steven smiled ruefully. "How many points do you get on the ol' Jerk-o-meter, Jess?"

"This one goes right off the scale, Steven," Jessica replied seriously. "Listen," she said. "Maybe it's time we called a truce, big brother. When you think of all Melissa and Andy have been through, this fight seems pretty stupid."

Steven nodded in agreement. "What *were* we fighting about, anyway?"

"I forget." Jessica shrugged. "But I'm sure you started it!"

Elizabeth stood. "Well, at least something good's come out of this mess." She gave Mr. Wakefield a hug. "Thanks for all your help tonight, Dad."

"There's not much more I can do until Andy's trial, I'm afraid," Mr. Wakefield said. "Why don't you try to get some sleep, honey? In fact, why don't we all get to bed? It's been a long night."

Jessica followed Elizabeth up the stairs. "Lizzie," she said softly when they reached the top, "I'm sorry I wasn't more of a help." She looked away, tapping her finger on the banister. "You want to know the truth? I think the whole thing with Melissa's mom really scared me more than I wanted to admit. I didn't want to even think about what she's going through. I'm glad she had someone like you to help her out."

"A lot of good I did," Elizabeth said.

"You can't blame yourself, Elizabeth."

But Elizabeth couldn't help it. For long hours she lay awake, thinking of poor Melissa lying in some strange bed with no brother, no parents, nothing.

Then it hit her. A wonderful, crazy, impossible idea. It was a long shot, but what did they have to lose?

Melissa had already lost everything that mattered to her.

"What are you doing, Elizabeth?" Jessica asked, walking into her twin's room the next morning. "It's Saturday. Don't you know you're supposed to sleep in?"

Elizabeth looked up from the envelope she was addressing. "I couldn't sleep."

"You're not working on the social studies project, are you?"

"In a way," Elizabeth replied. "At least I hope I am."

Jessica yawned. She leaned over Elizabeth's shoulder and read the address on the envelope. "Lone Star Motel," she read. "Who do you know in Texas?"

"No one." Elizabeth licked a stamp and placed it on the envelope. She looked up at Jessica and crossed her fingers. "Not yet, anyway."

Fourteen

The first thing Melissa saw when her social worker, Ms. Scott, drove her home a week later was the rose bush. It drooped sadly, peach rose petals carpeting the ground beneath it.

Then she saw Andy. He was standing in the driveway, waiting for her, just as Ms. Scott had promised. She'd called Andy's foster mother and arranged for them to meet here, since Melissa and Andy both needed to pick up some more clothes.

Melissa had been grateful to Ms. Scott for the chance to see Andy for a few minutes. They'd spoken every day on the phone, but this would be the first time since his arrest that they'd actually been together.

Now, as she stepped out of the car, Melissa wondered if they'd made a mistake. She didn't think she could bear to hug Andy one last time, only to watch him disappear again.

"Lissa?" Andy called.

The sound of his voice sent Melissa running. They embraced, tears streaming down Melissa's cheeks.

"I'm sorry, Lissa," Andy said. "I'm so sorry. I didn't want to do it, believe me. I thought I didn't have any choice."

"It's OK," Melissa sobbed. "We tried, Andy. We tried as hard as we could."

They sat down on the porch steps. "Are they treating you OK?" Andy asked. "Do you need anything?"

Melissa shook her head. *Only you*, she thought to herself. She brushed away her tears with the back of her hand.

"Mr. Wakefield's a good lawyer, Andy," she said, forcing hope into her voice. "Maybe . . ." She stopped herself. She knew better than to hope anymore.

Melissa watched as a battered blue car pulled to a stop across the street. She looked over at Ms. Scott and Andy's foster mother chatting at the end of the driveway.

"Mr. Franco's roses," Melissa said softly. "Just look at them. I hope he understands."

"Do you understand?" Andy asked, choking back emotion. "Can you forgive me?"

"There's nothing to—"

Melissa stopped in mid-sentence. Suddenly, she'd forgotten how to breathe, or talk, or think.

A man was getting out of the blue car. He was carrying a letter in one hand. Melissa blinked and looked again. The backseat of his car was piled high with belongings. And on the top of the pile was a beautiful, shiny guitar.

"Andy?" she said, her voice shaking.

Andy didn't answer.

The man was walking up the driveway in slow, measured steps.

"Andy?" Melissa whispered again.

"I know," he whispered back.

Melissa sat, trembling, until she couldn't wait any more. Then she ran to her father and hugged him close, never wanting to let go.

"What a great day for a pool party," Elizabeth said happily.

Melissa grinned. "It is a great day." She glanced over at the other end of the patio, where Mr. and Mrs. Wakefield were talking to Mr. McCormick. "How can I ever thank you, Elizabeth?"

"You *have* thanked me," Elizabeth reminded her. "About a thousand times in the past week!"

"I keep thinking that if you hadn't written that letter . . ." Melissa's voice trailed off.

"Don't think about that now," Elizabeth told

her. "You've got too much good news to think about, now that they've dropped the charges against Andy."

"Your dad's a great lawyer," Melissa said.

"Hey, kids," Mrs. Wakefield said, waving. "Come over here. Mr. McCormick brought his guitar. He's going to sing a song for us."

When everyone had gathered around, Mr. McCormick tuned up the guitar and strummed a few notes. "I'd like to dedicate this song to Elizabeth," he said, sending her a smile. "If it weren't for her, I might not be here today with the two people I love most in the world." He cleared his throat, blinking back tears. "I was afraid I'd lost them for good."

Elizabeth saw Melissa smile at Andy and felt a wonderful sense of relief wash over her. She looked over at Steven and Jessica sitting together on a deck chair.

"This song is called 'Sierra Lullaby,' " Mr. McCormick said as he plucked a chord. "I used to sing it to Melissa when she was a little girl. Back then, I was sure I would make it big some day."

He looked at Melissa and Andy. "And now I finally have."

"I wonder where Andy went," Melissa said. She, Elizabeth, Jessica, and Lila were lying back on the patio after having stuffed themselves with grilled hamburgers and ice cream.

"He's in the driveway with Steven and Joe shooting baskets," Elizabeth answered.

"He can't wait to catch up on his schoolwork and get back on the team," Melissa said.

"Hey, speaking of schoolwork," Elizabeth said. "We'd better get going on our families project."

"It was nice of Mrs. Arnette to give us extra time," Melissa said.

"Mrs. Arnette? Nice?" Jessica cried.

"If Mrs. Arnette were nice, would she have given Jessica a C minus on her families report?" Lila asked.

"It *was* only a page long," Elizabeth commented.

"Lila has a small family," Jessica pouted. "There wasn't much to say."

Melissa smiled at her father across the patio. "Well, I have a small family, too, but believe me, Elizabeth's going to have plenty to write about."

Everyone laughed. "You guys better hurry up with that project," Jessica warned. "Next week we start on the pioneer stuff with that new student teacher."

"I can't wait," Lila said. "Student teachers are always a joke. We'll get away with murder."

"Who knows?" Elizabeth said. "We might even like her."

"Elizabeth," Jessica chided. "You're such an optimist."

Find out what the mystery teacher has in store for the sixth grade in Sweet Valley Twins and Friends #59, BARNYARD BATTLE.

Join Jessica and Elizabeth for
big adventure in exciting
SWEET VALLEY TWINS SUPER EDITIONS
and SWEET VALLEY TWINS CHILLERS.

☐ #1: CLASS TRIP   15588-1/$3.50

☐ #2: HOLIDAY MISCHIEF   15641-1/$3.50

☐ #3: THE BIG CAMP SECRET   15707-8/$3.50

☐ #4: THE UNICORNS GO HAWAIIAN   15948-8/$3.50

☐ SWEET VALLEY TWINS SUPER SUMMER
   FUN BOOK by Laurie Pascal Wenk   15816-3/$3.50

Elizabeth shares her favorite summer projects &
Jessica gives you pointers on parties. Plus:
fashion tips, space to record your favorite
summer activities, quizzes, puzzles, a summer
calendar, photo album, scrapbook, address book
& more!

CHILLERS

☐ #1: THE CHRISTMAS GHOST   15767-1/$3.50

☐ #2: THE GHOST IN THE GRAVEYARD

                                                            15801-5/$3.50

☐ #3: THE CARNIVAL GHOST   15859-7/$2.95

- -

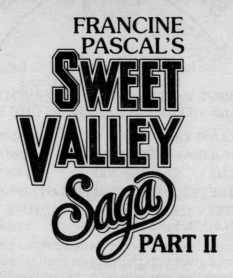

☐	27567-4	**DOUBLE LOVE #1**	$2.95
☐	27578-X	**SECRETS #2**	$2.99
☐	27669-7	**PLAYING WITH FIRE #3**	$2.99
☐	27493-7	**POWER PLAY #4**	$2.99
☐	27568-2	**ALL NIGHT LONG #5**	$2.99
☐	27741-3	**DANGEROUS LOVE #6**	$2.99
☐	27672-7	**DEAR SISTER #7**	$2.99
☐	27569-0	**HEARTBREAKER #8**	$2.99
☐	27878-9	**RACING HEARTS #9**	$2.99
☐	27668-9	**WRONG KIND OF GIRL #10**	$2.95
☐	27941-6	**TOO GOOD TO BE TRUE #11**	$2.99
☐	27755-3	**WHEN LOVE DIES #12**	$2.95
☐	27877-0	**KIDNAPPED #13**	$2.99
☐	27939-4	**DECEPTIONS #14**	$2.95
☐	27940-5	**PROMISES #15**	$3.25
☐	27431-7	**RAGS TO RICHES #16**	$2.95
☐	27931-9	**LOVE LETTERS #17**	$2.95
☐	27444-9	**HEAD OVER HEELS #18**	$2.95
☐	27589-5	**SHOWDOWN #19**	$2.95
☐	27454-6	**CRASH LANDING! #20**	$2.99
☐	27566-6	**RUNAWAY #21**	$2.99
☐	27952-1	**TOO MUCH IN LOVE #22**	$2.99
☐	27951-3	**SAY GOODBYE #23**	$2.99
☐	27492-9	**MEMORIES #24**	$2.99
☐	27944-0	**NOWHERE TO RUN #25**	$2.99
☐	27670-0	**HOSTAGE #26**	$2.95
☐	27885-1	**LOVESTRUCK #27**	$2.99
☐	28087-2	**ALONE IN THE CROWD #28**	$2.99

Buy them at your local bookstore or use this page to order.

Bantam Books, Dept. SVH, 2451 South Wolf Road, Des Plaines, IL 60018

Please send me the items I have checked above. I am enclosing $_____
(please add $2.50 to cover postage and handling). Send check or money
order, no cash or C.O.D.s please.

Mr/Ms _____

Address _____

City/State _____ Zip _____

Please allow four to six weeks for delivery.
Prices and availability subject to change without notice.

SVH–3/92